CHILDREN OF THE VOICE 2

By the same author:

The History of Ishmael
Angels with Dirty Faces
Children of the Voice

Children
of the Voice 2

The Invasion of Newchurch

ISHMAEL

KINGSWAY PUBLICATIONS
EASTBOURNE

Front cover design by Vic Mitchell
Text illustrations by Johnny Gillett

British Library Cataloguing in Publication Data

Smale, Ian *1949–*
    Children of the voice 2.
    I. Title
    823.914 [J]

ISBN 0–86065–903–8

Printed in Great Britain for
KINGSWAY PUBLICATIONS LTD
1 St Anne's Road, Eastbourne, E. Sussex BN21 3UN by
Richard Clay Ltd, Bungay, Suffolk
Typeset by J&L Composition Ltd, Filey, North Yorkshire

Contents

I

The Party at Pig Hall

The night was dark and cold. The rain fell out of the sky with the force of a water cannon, while the wind blew in every direction like it was lost and trying to find its way home.

All the paths leading to Pig Hall were just soggy, gooey, filthy, dirty, squelchy, muddy tracks. Even the moon had gone back to bed and given up trying to shine. The only illumination was the occasional lightning flash across what was presumably the sky.

However, inside Pig Hall, everything was quite different. An enormous, gross, obese, ugly character (just to name a few of his more attractive features) was having his annual

7

bath in his swimming pool and singing at the top of his voice one of his favourite songs which went:

> All things dull and ugly
> All creatures greedy and fat
> All things stupid and horrible
> Yes, we have seen to that.

This hideous hulk was one of the Enemy Superpowers and went by the name of Greedy Gutrot.

Gutrot was obviously very excited, and the reason for that was simple. Tonight was party night at his place, and loads of his fiendish friends had agreed to come and have a lousy time celebrating their victories over the Voice.

Once Gutrot had finished washing all the parts that he could reach, which happened to be less than one tenth of his body, he rolled out of the water and lay under a drying machine he had stolen from a car-wash. He pressed a red button and let the warm air dry him off. Once dry, he had to find something to wear. For this special occasion he decided to put on his blue and white marquee tent kaftan.

With only an hour to go before his guests would arrive, he thought he would just go and inspect the tons of cold extra-greasy chips, and gallons of stale extra-sickly clotted cream, which he felt sure all would love to eat as it was so bad for them. But having no self-control he could not help himself eating at least three-quarters of his spread before anyone else arrived.

Then the doorbell rang and in came the mud splattered, soaking wet and grumbling Enemy Superpowers, and what a terrible bunch they were. Putrid Mouthful was the first to enter, having pushed Albina Spoiltbrat out of the way and left her lying face-down in the mud by the door. Putrid was his usual self, swearing, cursing and generally making all the air around him blue with his obscene language.

Joker Dirtbox, who was his close friend, soon pushed by everyone else to join Putrid in the blue-air zone. Then came Tara Weigh, Fester Fearfinder, Connie Fusion, Funnyboy Oddfellow (plus friend), and many many more.

The last to enter was someone nobody seemed to know, except Greedy Gutrot. He was followed by a large mobile cage. As all of the Superpowers didn't like listening and only wanted to talk about themselves, it was not surprising that no one talked to this foreign-looking stranger.

As the door of Pig Hall closed, the uncontrollable riot began. Having pushed past Gutrot without even saying hello, some made their way straight to the food and ate until they were ill. Others made their way to the cellar and started opening the taps of the enormous wine vats where Gutrot's infamous homebrew had been quietly fermenting for many years, and in no time had drunk themselves unconscious. The rest started spraying the walls with graffiti, and generally smashing up Pig Hall.

It only took an hour for all the Enemy Superpowers to be either worn out, blown out or thrown out by some of their own more aggressive counterparts. Then a strange quiet came over the whole place.

Greedy Gutrot had not joined in the festivities. He was much too large to run around the mansion, and he had been content just to sit and watch everyone else enjoying themselves. But now all was quiet he saw an opportunity to try to do something a little more constructive—like organise the destruction of the Children of the Voice rather than the furniture of Pig Hall.

With the help of one or two he passed the message around to all parts of the house that he wanted everyone to be in the main banqueting hall in five minutes. Although he got the expected arguments, moans and verbal abuse, everyone made it there because they were all a little bit wary of the fat freak's size.

'Have you all had a good time so far?' growled Gutrot, who decided to chair the meeting, as he was already filling up as much of the mammoth hall as everyone else put together. A few muffled comments followed which may have been, 'Great, boss, just the job,' or, 'Get lost, you big fat slob,' but he didn't really care what they thought. He had much more important things to share.

'Now listen here, my faithful and loyal Superpowers,' began Gutrot, as though he were speaking to intelligent beings. 'Oh, get on with it!' yelled an angry Des Ruption, who was standing on his chair and gesticulating with his body to try to get people to look at him instead of the chairman.

'Will you be quiet! Some of us would love to hear what is about to be said,' wimpered Creepy Bootlicker. 'I think that wonderful very generous Mr Gutrot is doing very well.' Then two opposing factions were formed and everyone started shouting out what they thought on the subject.

'Will you all shut up!' screamed Gutrot, who had now remembered that he was not talking to intelligent beings. Then he wobbled his enormous belly which left the floor, bounced on the ceiling making a noise like an amplified bass drum, and brought three chandeliers crashing to the floor.

Everyone quietened down.

'I have had reports from various sources on how we Enemy Superpowers are doing our job. The report is in three sections, so listen carefully.

'Firstly, our Nochurch Followers: these are doing very well. In fact I think we can all be very proud of ourselves, as the vast majority of people do see sense and like ourselves think the Voice has little or nothing to do with today's generation. We must notice how much more successful we have been in times of peace than in times of war. One of the reasons for this is that war makes them think of death and their future, whereas peace keeps them happily just thinking of the lovely fun they can have in the present.

'Oh, and don't forget, we must make sure that copies of the Voice's Manual are freely available; you see, when people can't get hold of it they want it, but when they have a copy, they never seem to bother to read it.

'Any questions?'

'Yeah,' they all shouted in unison, 'what about the Children of the Voice and this Newchurch?'

'I will mention them all in good time,' replied Greedy Gutrot, trying not to appear rattled, even though he hated hearing those words. No other questions followed.

'Secondly, our Oldchurch Followers. As I'm sure we are all aware, although there are thousands of Oldchurches, they will never grow any bigger, which is the beauty of them. Any new people who choose to join will only replace those who have had a change of heart and have decided to drop out and become part of Nochurch. Again, we must congratulate ourselves that we have been able to be such an influence on what at one time was thought to be a major threat to us. It's nice when our enemies become our allies.

'I do have one suggestion, however: we need to keep making them feel that they are doing well. May I suggest that although it is breaking all our rules we do allow them to plant a few new Oldchurches. This will be such a great encouragement to the faithful, and—bless them—they deserve it, don't they? Of course the overall attendances will remain the same—it's just that they will think they are expanding, when of course we all know that all they will really be doing is weakening their resources. From our point of view, a larger number of badly run Oldchurches will make our job even easier than it is now ... if that is possible.'

All the Enemy Superpowers burst out laughing. Now that was a real joke.

As the frivolity died down, again Gutrot asked if anyone had any questions.

'Yeah,' they all shouted together, 'what about the Children of the Voice and Newchurch?'

Greedy Gutrot was getting angry. 'I hate those words,' he bellowed. 'Life was so easy for all of us till they appeared.' Then he lowered his voice to the level of a whisper. 'But I have a cunning plan.'

At this a Superpower leapt up, thinking Gutrot was talking to him, and shouted, 'No I haven't!'

'Not you, stupid!' he snapped, remembering that one of his colleagues was called Cunning Plan. 'Anyway, it doesn't surprise me that you have no ideas. The last cunning plan you had was to encourage people to kill the Voice—and look how that backfired.'

'No, I have found a new friend with a cunning plan, someone you ignored when you all arrived and someone who is so intelligent that he has locked himself away all evening so he would not have to mix with you brainless rabble. He has come from another land where he has experienced a Littlekid's uprising before, and is able to give us some practical advice.'

Then with a loud voice Greedy Gutrot shouted, 'Enter Inventor!'

They all turned their eyes to the toilet door in the far left-hand corner of the hall with the 'Engaged' sign on it. They heard a rattling sound, and it was obvious the Inventor was having trouble working out how to undo the lock to make the engaged sign become vacant. But after five minutes, a short man with an almost bald head and thick spectacles appeared.

Gutrot continued, 'Ladies and Gentlemen, may I intro-duce you to Professor Mindwarpt. A self-made, self-confessed genius.'

12

The other Superpowers responded by either shouting 'Rubbish!' or blowing raspberries, which was of course their usual way of honouring someone.

The Professor thanked them for their warm welcome and then went on to congratuate them on their job well done in both Nochurch and Oldchurch. 'Your reputations are known planetwide. You are indeed masters of your trades.' This was music to the Enemy Superpowers' ears; they loved it and started to pat themselves on their own backs and hug themselves in self-adoration.

'But,' continued Mindwarpt, 'with the Children of the Voice and Newchurch you guys are ... dated, ineffectual and useless. In short, history!'

The Superpowers were furious and started cheering and shouting hooray as was their usual response to those they disagreed with, and it wasn't until Gutrot again threw his massive stomach ceilingward, this time cracking it and showering everyone with plaster, that they all quietened down.

'Hear me out,' said the agitated Mindwarpt. 'This Newchurch is young. In a few years' time you could be back in business again. But right now you are all far too obvious to them. They are too committed to the Voice to fall for your little ploys of using bad language, telling dirty jokes, having bad friendships, or being scared or greedy. You are all too blatant. But I have a plan. I am going to introduce the Children of the Voice to my own created Superpowers ... the Mindwarpt Superbreed.'

Mindwarpt's large cage entered the room by remote control, as if by magic, with six coffin-type boxes in it.

Mindwarpt walked over to the cage with a half-smile and a half-sneer as he could see the other Superpowers who were so shocked their eyes were popping out.

13

'Inside each coffin,' he snarled, 'is a counterfeit Littlekid which looks like the real thing, will sound like the real thing, but is not the real thing. Each one is a masterpiece, skilfully crafted by me and under my personal control. They are robots that will destroy once and for all the Children of the Voice.'

The other Superpowers continued gasping until one shouted out that he wanted to see them.

'You fool!' stormed the Professor. 'You will not see, or know the identity, of any one of my magnificent six. Why do you think I've caged them in a impregnable cage? It's not so they won't get out; it is so no one will be able to get in to see them.

'Their identity will remain the most closely guarded secret since the ingredients of the Kentucky Fried Chicken.' Gutrot licked his lips at the thought. 'At the right time I will release each one of my Littlekid Superbreeds to infiltrate Newchurch, and within a year Newchurch will be back in our control.'

The Enemy Superpowers again started blowing raspberries and spitting in sheer enthusiasm, until one lonely voice shouted the words, 'What about Little Christian?'

All went deathly quiet.

Greedy Gutrot smiled. 'I have heard a rumour from a very reliable source that Little Christian is being given a job which, would you believe, will take him away from Newchurch for a year. By that time there will not only be no Newchurch, there will also be no Little Christian. I hate that Littlekid, and I am going to make it my job to see he's put out of action ... for keeps.'

With this all the Enemy Superpowers went wild. In joy they started smashing up all the furniture, ripping off the roof, then pulling down the walls.

As dawn came, all was quiet, although the rain still

poured down. The Enemy Superpowers had gone back to their evil deeds; the Professor and his cage had disappeared, even Greedy Gutrot had left, and all that was left of Pig Hall was a pile of wood and rubble.

2
First Call—Last Breath

Little Christian sat in his office glancing down at the computer printout of his diary. It was hard to imagine that Newchurch had only been in action for one year; so much seemed to have happened. For him it had been quite an easy year with a few minor hiccups but no major disasters.

It was so encouraging to see that so many Littlekids had come to join them, having been rescued from the Bigwideworld, but although they had a few adults return from the Voices Training Module, still very few older adults wanted to leave Oldchurch or Nochurch to join them. He guessed that the main reason for many not joining them was that they were not willing to be part of a church where their leaders were younger than they were.

Putting his diary to one side he picked up two of his Voice-Fax sheets. These were now a few months old, but he refused to put them in the rubbish bin.

One was from Hearthunter who had returned to Cross-country and contacted him to let him know he was busier than he ever had been. The other was from Miraclekid, who, apart from starting a school of training for other Miraclekids, also had some wonderful stories of the super-natural battles he had been involved in.

Putting the Voice-Faxes to one side he reflected on how pleased he had been with Buddy and Harmony; they really had taken over looking after the Newchurch Family.

Then (instinctively whenever he started thinking about his old friends) he looked down at a photo on his desk. Two thirteen-year-olds with their arms round each other, laughing like there was no problem in the world. 'That was eleven months ago,' he thought. 'The last picture taken of Angela and me before she was called on another Commission.'

Little Christian was missing her like mad, but he knew that being Children of the Voice, both he and Angela must put the Voice first in their lives and be obedient to him.

But why hadn't she been in touch for nearly a year?

His concentration was broken by a knock at the door, and a cheerful Littlekid entered dressed in brightly coloured shorts, kneepads, elbowpads, a helmet and worn-out trainers with attaching olly flaps.

'Hi, you must be Little Christian,' said the smiley face. 'I'm Rhoda Skateboard. I'm learning how to be a messenger from the Voice, and I've come straight from the Training Module with this sealed envelope to deliver to you personally.'

Little Christian thanked her, but couldn't help being surprised at the fact that the Voice seemed to be giving responsibilities to younger and younger Littlekids. As he looked at the envelope he saw that the Voice's seal had been broken.

'Um, Rhoda,' he said, not meaning to sound too accusing, 'you haven't by any chance opened up the envelope for any reason, have you?'

Rhoda looked stunned. 'Certainly not!' she cried. 'Who do you think I am to even consider that I would do such a thing?'

Little Christian could see that she was getting upset but still felt that he had to find out why it was open. 'I'm sorry, Rhoda,' he said. 'I didn't mean to sound like I didn't trust you, but ...' Then he thought for a moment. 'You didn't by any chance stop at all between the Training Module and here, did you?'

She thought for a moment then said, 'No, I came straight here, that is, I almost came straight here. I did just stop for a few minutes when I passed a skateboard park that was full of the most wonderful ramps I have ever seen, and a kind person invited me in to have a go at some drop-ins for free. But it was only for a few minutes.'

'I see,' said Little Christian. And did you let go of the envelope?

'Oh yes,' replied Rhoda. I mean, have you ever tried to negotiate those ramps with your hands full? It's just not possible, you know.'

Just as Rhoda began to get very excited about the skateboard park, Little Christian cut in and asked her what the kind man looked like.

'Oh, he was amazing,' said Rhoda. 'He was absolutely enormous, but very kind.'

'Thank you, Rhoda. That will be all. You had better go now because I'm sure you have more work to do; but take my advice—in future don't be distracted from what the Voice tells you to do, even if it *is* a skateboard park.'

'OK,' said Rhoda, 'I'll do my best. See you around.' And off she went, closing the door behind her.

Little Christian stood up and walked around the room, quietly seething. 'So after a year of not hearing from him, Gutrot is still alive and sick, even trapping little girls now,' he thought out loud as he took the contents out of the envelope and saw that it contained a photomap and a note.

The note went as follows:

Little Christian, I have a Commission for you.

For one year now you have been leading Newchurch. It is now time for you to leave them for a while to make sure that they don't just look to you ... but that they learn to look to me. They are also getting to the point where they still expect you to do things for them that by now they ought to know how to do themselves.

With this in mind, I want you to follow my photomap to a place called Deadbody. Here you will find some Voice followers who still have some life in them. They have chosen to be trapped there for various reasons. I want you to tell them all about Newchurch; then maybe they will hear what you are saying and choose to come and live, rather than stay where they are and eventually die.

Be warned, your route is not easy. The Enemy Superpowers have you on their hitlist. I will however be with you and will also be sending you a partner because, as you know, I do not commission people individually but in pairs.

Your Friend,
The Voice.

Little Christian put the photomap and letter down, then picked up a copy of the Manual to compare the handwriting and check that the letter was genuine, not a fraud. Then when he saw it was from the Voice he fell on his knees and, using a language that only the Voice understood, gave thanks to him. He also prayed that the Voice would tell him who his partner would be, but the Voice told him to be patient and to wait and see.

As Little Christian left his office he was filled with excitement and spontaneously burst into song:

> All people have a choice,
> But we are children of the Voice.
> Please help us to be faithful to the end.
> Our commission now we know
> When the Voice says 'go,' we'll go,
> For the Voice will always be
> The childrens' friend.

All the other Littlekids and adults who passed by also felt as excited as he did, and within no time at all everyone in Newchurch was singing along with Little Christian, even though very few knew why Little Christian was celebrating.

As the singing continued, the darkness of the night began to fall like a huge umbrella. The warm air soon made way for the chilling breeze; then this in turn had to give way to the authority of cold and frost.

As the singing subsided and Newchurch folk were snuggled up in their warm beds, no one was aware of a thin, badly beaten Littlekid who scarcely had the strength to drag her bruised and bleeding body over the razor sharp rocks of the Bigwideworld.

Her body was permanently shivering, and all that she had covering her was a vest and a ripped pair of jeans. Her bare feet were red from the cuts, brown from the mud and blue from the cold.

Little Christian was so excited about his Commission that he had lost all sense of tiredness. He thought he would watch the television, but all he could pick up was depressing programmes from Nochurch and Oldchurch. Then he thought that he would go and visit someone, but then he couldn't make his mind up whom to go and see. In the end he thought he heard a voice in his mind instructing him to go for a walk, and as nothing else had come to mind this seemed like a good idea.

He had read in the Manual that the Voice had often gone onto lonely hills at night to pray, and so rather than just walk around Newchurch, he decided to put on his big warm coat, grab a torch and take a stroll over the hills of the Bigwideworld.

The little girl knew that she could go no farther. She had never stopped talking to the Voice, and her spirit was strong, but her body was giving up on her. A thought flashed through her mind that maybe the Voice was calling her home; perhaps now was the time that she was going to enter into the for ever, and to be always with him. She had no fear of death because she was one of the Children of the Voice.

Her last movement was to pull herself onto a high rock, and even though her eyes were very blurred she thought she could just make out the lights coming from Newchurch, so near yet so far. She allowed her eyes to close and pulled her thin little legs up to her chin to try and get a bit more warmth. Then with her last few lungfuls of breath she started singing in a gentle whisper:

There is no one else around
In the air or on the ground
Who has the power (has the power) of the Voice.
So you Enemy Superpowers
In your defeated final hours
We command you to leave—you have no choice (you have
    no choice)
As we speak in the authority of the . . .

Then her voice went quiet.

Suddenly a bright glare of a torch-beam shone straight into her face. 'Angela!' screamed Little Christian, his eyes filling with tears and staring in unbelief at the freezing little body huddled on the rock. 'Is that you?' The little girl gave a faint smile ... then stopped breathing.

3
Gone but Not Forgotten

Very carefully, with tears running down his cheeks, Little Christian put his coat over Angela and picked up her limp little body. As fast as he could he rushed back to Newchurch. Then after putting the body on his bed he ran around waking everybody up, telling them about her.

The doctor was the first to see Angela. Having taken just one glance at her, he shook his head, then he checked her pulse and heartbeat, and looking up at Little Christian the sad doctor quietly informed him he was sorry but she was now in the hands of the Voice.

Everyone was heartbroken. They all knew that the Voice

sometimes used doctors and sometimes just did the healing himself, without doctors; but here nothing could be done; it was too late and they had no suggestions or answers.

Buddy and Harmony tried to comfort the shattered Little Christian, but no words they could say seemed to help. All the excitement of the day had gone. Now was a time of mourning and sadness.

Eventually everyone went to bed, all except Little Christian who simply sat in his office sobbing and sobbing, looking at the photo on his desk. He accidentally knocked his Manual off his desk and it fell open on the floor, but he failed to notice it. In fact within a few hours he too had fallen asleep on the floor next to it. His eyes, all red, had run dry of tears.

At about seven o'clock, he could hear the birds singing as the sun began to shine through his window, but even under the warm rays that woke him he didn't want to stir. In fact he didn't want to do anything.

It was then that the door swung open and all Little Christian's burning eyes could see was the bright light glaring at him.

'Get up, Little Christian,' came a command from the doorway.

Little Christian leapt to his feet. He'd recognise that voice anywhere. 'Miraclekid, is that really you?' he stammered.

'Of course it is, Little Christian, but why are you lying on the floor when you have work to do?'

As Little Christian ran over to give Miraclekid a hug he told him to sit down as he had some sad news to tell him about Angela.

Miraclekid allowed Little Christian to tell him the whole story, and when he had finished Miraclekid stared at him. 'Did you think of asking the Voice what was going on?' he said.

'Why,' said Little Christian. 'What's the point of asking the Voice questions about a dead person? She's gone, it's over.'

'The Voice must have tried to speak to you last night. Have a look at where your Manual fell open at.'

Little Christian picked up his Manual and read how the Voice had brought a little girl back from the dead. 'Yes, but that was all very well when the Voice was walking around on the face of this earth, but that doesn't happen today ... does it?'

'It's funny, you know, you remind me of someone from Oldchurch, not Newchurch,' said Miraclekid. 'Listen, get it into your mind that the Voice is as powerful today as he ever was. In fact, doesn't the Manual tell us that even greater things are going to happen in our generation?'

Little Christian just hung his head and went red with embarrassment at his unbelief.

'Obviously not everybody will be raised from the dead,' Miraclekid continued, getting into his preaching mode, 'or else the Voice would have no one living with him now, but Angela was sent here to be your partner for your Commission, so it's not very likely that she's gonna stay dead, is it?'

'But I never guessed that she was going to be my partner. The Voice never told me,' protested Little Christian.

'Well, fair enough,' said Miraclekid, rapidly running out of answers. 'Nobody understands everything the Voice does or why he does things in his way, but we do know that he has a perfect plan and that everything he does is for the best. I'm sure he had a reason for not telling you. . . .' Then after a moment's thought he continued, 'Come to think of it, if he had told you, there would have been no reason for me being here. Anyway, come on, let's go and wake her up. She has been asleep long enough.'

They left Little Christian's office and on the way to Little Christian's house Miraclekid stopped at the café and asked them to prepare a nice big hot breakfast for Angela. 'She'll need that,' he said.

Little Christian didn't dare say a word as his faith was still rather low. He was still trying to work out if he was about to see a great miracle, or a great embarrassment thanks to this over-zealous nutcase of a friend.

As they entered the bedroom, Angela lay cold and still on his bed, just as she had been when Little Christian left her the night before. 'Cor, she's in a bit of a state, isn't she?' said Miraclekid.

'She's dead,' replied Little Christian sadly.

'No, she's just asleep.' Miraclekid looked at Angela and with a voice of authority that sounded like thunder commanded life back into the body, in the name of the Voice.

Immediately, Angela's eyes started to twitch. Then they opened a fraction. Then they burst open wide, and a big smile spread across her face. Miraclekid and Little Christian fell flat on the floor as they began to realise just how powerful the Voice is.

'He really has got the power over life and death!' shouted Little Christian, and after a time of giving thanks he jumped up and ran to hug Angela.

'Go gently,' said Miraclekid. 'She's very weak, and she hasn't had her breakfast yet.' Looking out of the window, he remembered that he hadn't had his, either, and he wished he had ordered one for himself as well.

Angela hadn't yet said anything. When the doctor was brought in, he explained that although he had never seen a miracle like it, Angela had still been through a terrible ordeal and needed to rest for a few days to get her strength back. Miraclekid of course didn't agree with the doctor, but Little Christian, Buddy and Harmony did; so Miraclekid reluctantly watched as Angela was taken by a praising group of Littlekids into the Newchurch hospital.

'What about her breakfast?' shouted Little Christian, but when he turned round he noticed that Miraclekid had quickly disappeared into the café and was already halfway through it. Everyone burst out laughing.

After he'd eaten, Miraclekid shouted goodbye to everyone, then turning to Little Christian gave him a hug and
told him he would see him soon.

'Don't go without saying goodbye to Angela, will you?'
said Little Christian.

Miraclekid didn't like the thought of that; the two things
he did not relate to were hospitals and girls, but he felt he
ought to see her before he went.

Gingerly he crept up to the door, then poked his head
round and saw Angela lying there. 'Bye, Angela,' he
whispered.

She signalled with her hand that he should come over to
her bedside, which he did. Then she started opening her
mouth like she was trying to say something, but he couldn't
make out what she was saying, so he put his ear close to her
lips. It was then that Angela cunningly moved her head to
one side and gave him a great big kiss on his cheek. 'Thank
you,' she whispered.

Miraclekid shot up in the air as if he had sat on a stinging
nettle with short trousers on. 'Oh, think nothing of it,
Angela. After all, I was only obeying the Voice. See you
around.' And with that he raced out of the door.

Little Christian was waiting outside the door. 'Is she any
better?' he enquired.

'Oh, I think she'll pull through,' said the red-faced
Miraclekid as he raced off back towards the Bigwideworld.
'Well, her lips seem to work anyway,' he shouted. 'See ya.'

Little Christian burst out laughing again, guessing what
Angela had done. 'She must be improving. It didn't take her
long to get back to her usual little old cheeky self,' he
thought.

Within a very short time Angela regained not just her
humour but also her strength, even though she seemed a lot
thinner than she used to be. Little Christian showed her the
letter from the Voice and the photomap to Deadbody, and

although she listened intently, she said very little. She still had her wonderful strange accent, but for most of the time she would only say words like 'yeah' and 'no' and 'maybe,' and didn't really seem to be able to enter into a conversation.

Little Christian kept asking her to tell him about how and why she was in such a bad state when he found her, but somehow either Angela couldn't or wouldn't talk about it. Sometimes she'd say that her mind had gone blank and she could not recall what had happened; then on other occasions she'd say it was too painful to think about it, and could they change the subject.

Little Christian wanted to help her. He knew that she needed it, but this could only happen when she was ready to receive his help. There would be a time when all that had happened would come out into the open and he would have to be prepared for when that time came.

Angela had been in Newchurch for fourteen days, and one day when she and Little Christian were in the office studying the Manual together there was a knock on the door. In walked Rhoda Skateboard all decked out in her usual attire.

'Hello, Rhoda,' said Little Christian. Then after introducing Rhoda to Angela he was given an envelope from the Voice. Seeing that the seal had not been broken this time, he winked at Rhoda and she smiled back. 'Yippee!' yelled Little Christian, dancing around the table as he read the letter. 'We are off this afternoon.'

They all danced around the table together, even though Rhoda didn't have a clue what they were on about. She was a little sad when they explained to her where they were going, especially because the Voice had told her that he wanted her to come off deliveries for a bit and spend some time being trained in Newchurch. Now just as she arrived the leaders were going!

'Don't worry about that,' said Little Christian. 'Buddy

and Harmony have been here with me since the beginning, and they will train you well.'

Little Christian and Angela packed a few essentials and went round saying goodbye to everyone.

Little Christian was still concerned about the lack of strong leaders in Newchurch. It was not that they had failed to train new leaders; it was just that a year is a very short time for people to come from the old and be leading in the new. Were they really ready and able to take on more responsibility? Buddy and Harmony were great, but with Angela and him away, the only other strong ones who could really take his place were Hearthunter and Miraclekid, and they too were out on Commissions and not available.

Buddy and Harmony tried to reassure him that everything would be fine. 'There are a lot of up-and-coming new leaders,' Buddy explained. 'Who knows?' he said, smiling, 'the Voice might even send in one or two mature ones after you have gone.'

After lunch everybody in Newchurch came out to wave goodbye as their dynamic duo set out for Deadbody. Harmony had promised to look after Rhoda and had taken both her and her skateboard into her lodgings, while the other local leaders had promised to support both Harmony and Buddy in taking care of Newchurch.

The last words they heard from Newchurch came from Buddy as he shouted, 'Try not to be away too long. Remember this will always be your home.'

Unseen by anyone, from behind a rock came an evil chuckle that nobody heard. 'You mean this *was* your home,' the evil voice whispered as he unlocked the largest coffin. An imitation Littlekid stepped out.

'Welcome to my world,' said Professor Mindwarpt.

'Thank you, O Mighty Supervoice,' the Littlekid replied.

'Oh, I love that title,' said the Professor, chuckling. Then he continued, 'I have made you very wise and clever, and

I've created you to be the very best leader. No other leader will ever match up to you. Everyone will be your servant . . . but you must do everything I say.'

'I will obey you, O Mighty Supervoice,' replied the Littlekid.

'Good,' said Mindwarpt. 'And remember, you are bugged so I will hear every word you say. I will be with you always, so watch it. If I notice any foul-ups with your obeying system you will be terminated immediately. Is that understood?'

'Loud and clear, O Mighty Supervoice,' came the reply.

'Now, what shall I call you? Yes, I know. I'll call you Shepherd, and because you are the largest and weigh more than any other of my superbreeds, your first name will be Heavy. Yes, off you go, and do your worst, young Heavy Shepherd.'

4

A Buddy for Buddy

The sun was shining down, and it was a lovely warm day to start a Commission. Both Angela and Little Christian were very excited about what they had been called to do.

'Hey, Angela, what do you know about this first place we are due to call at? It's called Treasure Iceland.'

'Do wot?' said Angela. 'Never 'erd of it, but if it's as nice as wot it is 'ere, I ain't gonna grumble.'

'Well it's a few kilometres from here yet,' said Little Christian. 'So in case it's not, enjoy this while you can.'

Meanwhile, Buddy felt a bit sad with Little Christian gone, and deep down he wondered how he would cope without him. He made his way over to Little Christian's office, which he would from now on use as his own, till Little Christian returned. There he sat down behind the desk and found himself staring at the photo of Little Christian and Angela. He thought as he began to clear the desk-top that maybe he would put it away somewhere, but then he decided he would leave it in front of him. It would be a reminder to pray for them regularly.

As he continued clearing papers away, a head came peering around the door. 'Excuse me, may I come in?' the head asked. Buddy looked up and saw a rather large Littlekid facing him, one he didn't recognise. He was a bit embarrassed as he made it his duty to know everyone's name.

'Oh, yes, please do come in and take a seat,' he said. 'I'm ever so sorry, but I seem to have forgotten your name.'

'No, it's all right, you haven't forgotten my name,' smiled the Littlekid warmly. 'You see I'm new and have just arrived this afternoon. You have never met me before.'

Buddy felt relieved, and as the Littlekid sat down he poured him out a glass of orange juice. 'Ah, I'm sorry, but I don't touch fruit or vegetables. You see I believe that the Manual speaks very strongly about cruelty, and I believe that when a fruit is picked or vegetables cut up or dug up, they feel pain. They have both life and feeling, and I would not want to deprive them of either.'

'Very interesting,' said Buddy, getting rather confused, 'So then what do you eat?'

'Well,' said the Littlekid thoughtfully, 'I live on meat. After all, meat was put on the face of the earth for us to enjoy, and the Voice has even provided us with special teeth so that we can chew it properly. I'm a very strict meatatarian.'

'Well, you have certainly made some interesting points. I must remember that,' said Buddy. 'Now tell me, what is your name and where do you come from?'

The Littlekid explained that his name was Shepherd but his nickname was Heavy due to his size. Buddy cut in and said they wouldn't call him Heavy because it was cruel to make fun of people. 'Oh no, I love it,' said the Littlekid. 'Everyone calls me Heavy, and I'd like you to as well.'

'Very well,' said Buddy, 'if you insist.'

The Littlekid went on to explain that he had come from a brand new Voice's Training Module. Although he was lying the whole time he really impressed Buddy with his wisdom, his knowledge and his qualifications.

As he got up to leave, he could see that he had already surprised Buddy, as Buddy was getting very excited about him.

'It's amazing,' said Buddy, 'and of course you wouldn't know this, but this very afternoon our leader has been sent on a Commission and won't be back for a long while. I was wondering how I would cope, but it seems that the Voice knew all about that and he has sent you along just at the right time.'

'I don't know about that,' said Heavy in mock modesty. 'I have only come to serve. I believe it's only the humble ones who will be lifted up.'

This was music to Buddy's ears. *What a great attitude*, he thought. 'You and I, Heavy, are really going to see things change around here,' he shouted excitedly.

'Well, you know me, Buddy, whatever you want me to do I'll do it.' Then just as Heavy was walking out of the door he stopped and handed Buddy a piece of paper. 'If you get time, Buddy, perhaps you could check this out. They are all the reasons why people should be meatatarians.'

'I certainly will, Heavy,' said Buddy. 'If it means that much to you, there must be truth in it for all of us.'

Heavy Shepherd left the office feeling quite pleased with himself, but even more pleased with himself was a bald-headed Professor with spectacles, who although in hiding had tuned in to the whole conversation.

5

Treasure Iceland

'There it is,' said Little Christian, pointing to a snow-covered island about two kilometres out in the sea.

'Yeah, it must be, but why is it that we are standin' on this 'ot sandy beach, and that place—wot's only a little way away—is frozen solid?'

Although Little Christian had no answer to her question, he was thrilled that every hour Angela's sentences and comments were becoming more coherent and meaningful.

As they were considering how to get there, they heard a rumbling sound that seemed to be coming from the sea. The noise grew louder and louder as whatever it was got closer. Obviously it brought back a memory or fear into Angela's mind and she wanted to make a run for it, but Little Christian grabbed her hand firmly and reassured her that she had nothing to be afraid of as they were acting under the authority of the Voice.

Then they arrived. Driving straight out of the sea came six amphibious WarMachines with guns pointing out at every conceivable angle. On the roofs they had rockets and missiles, all with the most modern homing devices and technology imaginable.

The engines of the large vehicles stopped in unison as if someone had pulled their plugs out. Then an icy-cold voice came from the vehicle standing right in front of them. With menacing aggression the sound of the speaker echoed all over the bay. 'Who are you? What do you want, and do you realise you are trespassing by looking over at Treasure Iceland?'

Little Christian was not frightened by the WarMachine and shouted back to the vehicle, 'We have been sent by the Voice to visit you.' All went quiet for a moment, then an automatic door opened in the front of the machine from where the voice was coming. 'Enter,' it said coldly.

Little Christian and Angela walked down the hot sandy beach, then as they climbed in through the small door Angela accidentally touched the side of the vehicle and let out a little cry of pain.

'What's the matter?' asked Little Christian, who had climbed in first to make sure that everything was OK.

'I've just burned me finger on the side of the WarMachine,' she whispered.

'Surely it's not that hot?' argued Little Christian in disbelief.

'No, it's that cold,' replied Angela. 'It's literally frozen.'

The door of the WarMachine closed and they found themselves alone in a small compartment. It was a bit junky, like they were sitting in the middle of an old second-hand clothes shop. There were odd garments everywhere, and there were even what looked like old-fashioned diving suits in the corner. 'Not my idea of a trendy boutique,' commented Angela, and Little Christian nodded in agreement.

Then the sound of mighty engines started like the roar of an angry lion, and the machine reversed up then went crashing back into the sea again. Angela and Little Christian didn't bother to discuss their situation as the engines were so noisy that they couldn't even hear themselves think. It seemed like only minutes, though, before the engines cut out again.

'Oh no,' said Angela. 'I 'ate the thought of breakin' down in the middle of the sea.' But before she had finished her sentence, a voice ordered them to put on as many clothes as they could and then to put on the ice-repellent thermal suits in the corner. This they did without argument, as they guessed that what they were putting on was for their own protection. Then, when they were all togged up, the door by which they had entered opened again.

'Get out,' a voice commanded, 'and don't touch anything.'

They found it quite hard to walk with all the gear on, but more by falling out than climbing out they soon managed to leave the WarMachine. Even with all the clothes and the thermal suits, they still felt freezing and started to shiver with cold. But as they looked around they became intrigued at what they saw. They found themselves standing in a building that was not dissimilar to what Oldchurch used to call the church building or sanctuary. There were many seats all in lines, a box like a pulpit up the front and a large table at the front with a cross on it. But what was different from Oldchurch was that it was all made of snow and ice.

'Go and sit down,' said the voice from the WarMachine. They heard bells ringing and immediately the doors of the

WarMachine opened up as did many little doors all around the building.

Angela grabbed Little Christian's hand and gasped, 'I dun believe wot I'm seein',' she cried. 'Tell me it's not true.'

But it was true. In walked hundreds of adults and Littlekids, and all they were wearing were swimming costumes and sunglasses and nothing on their feet. They all sat down on the ice they were obviously all used to sitting on; then a person wearing black trunks, a sweatband and wristband walked up to the front and stood in the pulpit.

Without any warm word of welcome, he explained that he was sorry it was so hot this morning, but suggested the cause was the intrusion of these two Littlekids who claimed to come from the Voice. The man at the front used his wristband to wipe away the perspiration from his brow. 'Step up to the front,' he demanded. 'Say what you have to say, then we can get you off our island and bring the temperature back down to normal.'

Little Christian was not sure what to say, but Angela, who had been trained up as one of the Voice's directors, walked to the front, climbed into the freezing pulpit and began.

'The Voice 'as sent us to tell ya that 'e is very disappointed wiv ya. Many years ago you were warm, friendly people wot knew the warmf of the Voice's love, but now ye'r cold 'n' icy and even these subzero temperatures are too warm fer yer personalities to cope wiv.

'But worst of all,' she continued, 'the Voice is sad cos this island once contained rich treasures. Years ago you were some of the first people to discover the power of the Voice. Ya learned about 'is special language before most; ya saw 'ealings and miracles reg'ler, but ya chose to keep all the treasures fer yerselves on yer island and 'ated the thought of sharing 'em wiv others. That's why ye'r now the way ya are.'

Angela got down out of the pulpit and walked back to her

seat. Little Christian thought she was brilliant and started to give her a round of applause but soon stopped when he saw that everyone had turned round, and he felt all those cold eyes staring at him.

The speaker with the black trunks got back into his pulpit and looked hard at the two of them. 'We don't like girls speaking,' he said, 'and that includes those girls who unlike this one can speak properly. I was expecting the boy to speak, but obviously the girl is his mouthpiece.

'What the girl said, however, was totally predictable. We have heard it all before; in fact, every misguided speaker from the Voice seems to say the same thing. Why does everyone think that we are abnormal wearing our beachwear on our very own Treasure Iceland? I think they are abnormal, not us. Can any of you imagine what it would be like if you were warm and not as cold as the ice you are sitting on? Of course not. Surely we have something very special here, and this is the way that the Voice wants us to stay. No, I believe that the reason these so-called Voice speakers come over here is because they want us to hand over our treasure to them. No way! What is ours is ours by right, and no one else will have any of it.'

Everyone nodded in agreement.

'Finally, let today be yet another lesson to us. We must keep our Island well guarded. We must be ready to use our WarMachines, our guns and rockets so that we can protect what we have for us and our own Littlekids.'

The congregation started to applaud their great orator, but noticed that putting their hands together was causing warmth, so they soon stopped.

Little Christian leaped up. 'Hold on—you don't understand,' he screamed. 'You can't last for long. A global warming is happening right across the face of the planet, and your Treasure Iceland will be the first one to melt. You haven't got a future unless you are willing to change.'

'Rubbish!' everyone shouted together. 'That is impossible.'

Little Christian and Angela were told to get back into the WarMachine, then they were driven back to the mainland. As they walked up the beach a voice boomed out, 'If you are ever sighted even looking at Treasure Iceland again, you will be eliminated.' And with that threat the WarMachine disappeared back into the sea.

6

Unhappy Families

Professor Mindwarpt was just finishing bragging to his friend Greedy Gutrot about how successful Heavy Shepherd had been. 'It's even surprised me how gullible they are,' he joked. 'Can you believe it? He's already got Buddy to make a statement on how vegetables and fruit are bad for the Children of the Voice.'

'Excellent,' said Gutrot with a big grin. 'But don't count your chickens yet, Professor. Newchurch may seem weak at present, but they have some very strong allies drifting all over the Bigwideworld, and we want them destroyed as well.'

Mindwarpt took his friend's advice and decided it was time to send in two more of his superbreeds. He knew they would be a great support to Heavy Shepherd.

He opened the cage and took two more of the coffin lids off. There before him was a very attractive female and a good-looking male, and these two were a little older than Heavy Shepherd.

As both got out of their coffins, Mindwarpt commented on what a nice pair they made. Then he had a brainwave. 'Hold hands!' he ordered.

'Yes, O Mighty Supervoice,' they both replied.

'I pronounce you ... man and wife. You will enter Newchurch as a nice happy newly-married couple. Of course, I am not expecting you to act like you are married. I'm expecting you to wreck everyone else's idea of marriage,' he said, laughing. 'May I remind you that you are well and truly bugged and I will be listening in to all your conversations. So any hint of a malfunction, and I will terminate you both.'

'Yes, O Mighty Supervoice,' they again said together.

'Right, off you go to Newchurch and do your worst.'

Meanwhile, Little Christian and Angela were glad to be back on the mainland in the sunshine. Little Christian kept encouraging her about how clear her words had been when she was speaking from the Ice pulpit.

'Yeah,' said Angela, 'but do ya think I was right in doin' it? After all, 'e accused me of being yer mouthpiece.'

'Hey,' said Little Christian, 'I've got a big enough mouth of my own. If the Voice had given me something to say, I would have said it. But he chose to give you something to say so you were not my mouthpiece. You were the Voice's mouthpiece.'

'Well, y'er right about one fing,' said Angela thoughtfully.

'What's that?' asked Little Christian.

'Well, ya 'ave got a big mouth.' And she burst into laughter.

'You know something, I could really get to like you,' said Little Christian, half-joking.

'Then why don't ya?' replied Angela. Little Christian just grinned with embarrassment.

Heavy had been invited to move a desk in with Buddy and to share Little Christian's office so they could be more together in the work. To start with, Heavy had only had a small desk by the window. But as he needed more room to prepare, Buddy, being a very humble person, had offered him Little Christian's desk—which of course Heavy gratefully received.

The first time he was left alone in the office he tucked the photo of Little Christian and Angela into the desk drawer. Buddy did enquire about where it had gone, but Heavy convinced him that it was bad for him to keep looking at it as it would always keep him feeling inferior. Buddy tended to agree.

While Buddy was becoming close friends with Heavy, Harmony had become very close to Rhoda Skateboard, who was proving to be a wonderful little student. But Harmony still felt a bit left out when it came to more adult conversation. So you can imagine what a great thrill it was when a nice young married couple arrived on her doorstep with the hopes of becoming part of Newchurch. And they both seemed so friendly.

'And what are your names?' she asked.

'Well,' said the man, 'my name is Prophet. You see, I'm very much used by the Voice when it comes to sharing how he feels,' he lied.

'Great,' said a very excited Harmony. 'Your gift will be very welcome in Newchurch, but have you got a first name?'

'Well,' he said, 'it's a bit embarrassing, but when I was much younger I used to play a lot of ball games. The most amazing thing was that if someone ever tried to hit me, I always managed to dodge out of the way. Ever since then everyone's called me Dodgy.'

Dodgy then felt a whack on the shin. 'Don't forget me, darling,' said his wife, who had kept her mouth shut until then.

'Oh, I'm ever so sorry, Cherrylips. My wife, is a very shy lady. Only just got married, and here I am forgetting her already! Harmony, this is my wife, Lucy—Lucy Morals.'

'No it's not, silly,' said Lucy. 'We are married now, darling. My name is Lucy Morals Prophet.'

'Oh yes, of course it is, sugarlumps. You see her maiden name was Morals, but now of course she's a Prophet, like me.' He was now looking very embarrassed. 'So I suppose you could say that she's now become a Prophet but still likes to be called Lucy Morals. Is that right, pigeon pie?'

Lucy grinned furiously then gave him a massive kick on the other shin.

'Well, welcome to Newchurch, Dodgy Prophet and Lucy Morals. I'm sure we have a lot to offer you, and I'm sure you both have a lot to offer us,' said Harmony.

Dodgy, Lucy (and Professor Mindwarpt) grinned and agreed.

Within no time at all Dodgy was regularly speaking at meetings on behalf of the Voice, and although nearly everything he said was contrary to the Manual, because it got the full backing of Heavy Shepherd, nearly everyone was willing to agree with his teachings.

He also encouraged all the Littlekids to write down messages from the Voice for those they liked and those they didn't like. He explained that if they added the words 'so says the Voice' onto their message, people would take them a lot more seriously. Little notes were being passed around all the time, all claiming to be from the Voice, and within a very short time Newchurch couldn't remember what the real Voice sounded like.

Quiet, shy Lucy Morals, however, proved to be anything but quiet and shy! At the first meeting she went to she gently shook hands with both the men and women. In the second meeting she ignored the women and gave the men a warm embrace. By the third meeting she was embracing the men and kissing them on their cheeks—and so it went on. Funnily enough, she was only interested in the married men. The husbands played up to Lucy while the wives disliked her. She was beginning to accomplish her mission: she was already beginning to divide families.

Heavy Shepherd supported Lucy Morals all the way. He felt that she was a perfect example of real friendship and portrayed the love of the Voice. Many agreed with him, but many of the wives did not. He told the wives that they were being selfish and possessive and that Newchurch was one big family, not a lot of small ones. They must be willing to share everything and start being a real community. Heavy also thought she was very attractive, but he kept that to himself.

Buddy and Harmony were both in a bit of a state. Buddy could not agree with the way things were going; but he felt too weak and confused to oppose it, and his health was beginning to suffer. Harmony, on the other hand, just stayed more and more in her house feeling totally confused. Both knew that they were rapidly losing the respect and the leadership of Newchurch.

Late one night Rhoda felt like a break from her studying, so she decided she would go for a quick skateboard around the block. She knew that Harmony would not like her to be going out late, but she thought if she crept out quietly perhaps no one would notice. She crept down the stairs and saw a light in the living room, and as the door was slightly open she peeped in only to see Harmony fast asleep on the sofa.

Ever so quietly, she crept out of the door, then off she went down the road. All was quite dark and she guessed that everyone was in bed, but then she saw a light shining from the office window. 'Surely Buddy or Heavy can't be working this late?' She thought. 'I bet someone's left the light on. I'd better go and check.'

She crept over to the window very quietly, because if one of the leaders was working late she didn't want to be spotted and so get into trouble with Harmony.

Standing on tiptoes and looking in, she gasped in amazement at what she saw. Immediately she turned, dropped her skateboard and ran as fast as her little legs would carry her. 'How could they?' she sobbed. 'They are wicked and evil!' Rhoda crept back to her room knowing that after what she had seen she was not going to sleep a wink that night.

The office window opened and two heads looked out into the night. 'Well now, I guess we had better find the owner of that skateboard quickly,' said one.

'Yes,' said the other. 'And we must terminate the owner, before our owner terminates us.'

7

The Rotter Sets in

''Ow far is Deadbody from 'ere?' enquired Angela as she and Little Christian sat down exhausted under a large oak tree, with the sun still shining brightly overhead.

'Hold on—I'm just checking,' said Little Christian, carefully examining his photomap.

'Cor, we've 'arf come a long way,' she continued, looking over his shoulder.

'Yes, we have,' he agreed, looking down at his trainers and considering the aching feet inside them. 'Still, according to my calculations we should be reaching Deadbody within a couple of hours.'

'Thank goodness fer that,' said Angela, also looking down at her feet.

Still, something seems a little fishy, thought Little Christian to himself. Why haven't we actually met anyone since Treasure Iceland, which was ages ago? Where are all the wandering Littlekids. And more to the point, where is Greedy Gutrot and his gang?

As they got up and continued their journey, they passed through a small forest then came to a clearing. In the middle of the clearing they saw a huge notice-board with some tiny writing on it and a large arrow pointing to a small footpath which left the main track and went off to the left.

'Hey, what's this?' said Little Christian, running over to the board. Squinting his eyes, he could just about read what it said.

Before you go on ... you need to look back
If you want to progress ... you'll need to back-track
You'll need to retreat ... if you want to attack
Come learn of your history ... 'cause it's knowledge you
   lack.
Signed: The Vioce.

'Wow! It's a message from the Voice,' said Little Christian, failing to notice the spelling mistake in the signature. 'We'd better do as he says.'

'Wait a minute,' said Angela. 'This place ain't on our photomap. It may be a trap.'

'Oh don't be so suspicious,' laughed Little Christian. 'The Voice has probably just added this because there is something very strategic we need to know before we approach Deadbody. Now come on.'

Angela wasn't convinced, but she obediently followed her friend.

The path was winding and twisty and seemed to be going

on for ever. Then suddenly it stopped and they saw a 'DANGER—CLIFF EDGE' sign in front of them.

Carefully they moved towards the sign and could see a sheer drop in front of them which went down to a sort of quarry. 'Be careful,' said Angela, grabbing hold of his arm. 'Ye'r gettin' too near the edge.'

'No, I'll be all right,' replied Little Christian, moving even closer towards the drop.

'Gosh,' he shouted, 'I think that I can see a. . . .' And with that his words were cut short as the edge of the quarry that they were standing on crumbled away and both Little Christian and Angela went hurtling down the cliff-face, screaming as they fell.

Heavy Shepherd knocked loudly on the door, then as there was no answer he knocked even louder with great impatience. Eventually, the door opened and a very sleepy Harmony opened the door. 'Oh, hello, Heavy,' she said, glancing at her watch. 'This is rather late to be visiting, isn't it?'

Heavy pushed his way into the house. 'No, I'm afraid this is not a pastoral visit; this is something much more serious,' he said sternly. 'Newchurch is beginning to get out of hand due to our Littlekids severely lacking in discipline.'

'Well, I can't say that I have noticed it. Anyway, what has that got to do with me at this time of the night?' asked the perplexed Harmony.

'I'm afraid you are not bringing Rhoda Skateboard up in a way that is honouring to the Voice and our community. The girl is wild and rebellious. I have come to take her from you and put her in the hands of people I can trust.'

'But this can't be true,' said Harmony with tears welling up in her eyes. 'I've always taught her by the Manual, and she's been a wonderful Littlekid.'

'I have not come here to argue with you, Harmony. I am your leader and I know what's best. I want you to go and get her and her belongings and bring them to me now.'

Harmony started crying, 'But she's only a Littlekid. She won't understand. Who are you going to put her with?'

'Well, not that it is any of your business,' snapped Heavy, 'but if you must know she will be going to live with that highly respected couple Dodgy Prophet and Lucy Morals. They will bring her up in a way that I would be proud of.'

'No, I won't let you take her,' said Harmony, her tears turning to anger. 'Little Christian put her under my care and until he says differently, that's where she'll stay.'

'Little Christian, did I hear you say? Little Christian? Who on earth is he? Little Christian is just a bad memory; he won't be coming back here. I am your leader. No one else is, so you do what I say or face the consequences.'

'I refuse to obey you,' shouted Harmony, 'because I think you are wrong.'

Heavy roughly grabbed hold of her arm. His temper completely blown and with his eyes blazing, he stared straight into her face. With clenched teeth he whispered, 'Never, but never say that I am wrong. I am your leader, and I am never wrong.' Heavy turned to the door and gave a shout, then Dodgy and Lucy joined him in the house.

'Did you hear that wilful act of rebellion against her leader?'

Dodgy and Lucy nodded.

'Well,' he continued, 'according to my interpretation of the Manual, if there are two or three witnesses to rebellion we can take action.' Dodgy, I want you to take Harmony out of Newchurch and dump her in the middle of the Bigwideworld. From this moment, Harmony, you are banned—no, excommunicated—from Newchurch. Tomorrow I will announce your rebellion to the whole of my people and inform them that it will be a punishable offence for them in any way to communicate with you. In other words, don't even consider coming back here, because nobody will want to know you.'

Dodgy Prophet dragged Harmony out of the house and led her out into the darkness of the night.

'Well, Lucy, my dear,' said Heavy Shepherd, putting an arm around her, 'go and get your new little lodger and keep her locked up in a bedroom until we can think of a more permanent way to keep her mouth shut. And then,' he said with an evil grin, 'I will meet you back at my place in about an hour.'

8

A History Lesson

Angela opened one eye, then the other. She found herself staring into the face of a girl she had never seen before. 'Who are you?' she cried, sitting up and realising that she was on a bed.

'I'm Nurse Itbetter,' the girl replied, 'and this is my hospital. You had a nasty fall down into the quarry, you know. You're lucky that you didn't have any serious injuries. In fact your boyfriend's already up and about.'

'Me boyfriend? Oh, ya mean Little Christian,' Angela said with a smile. She felt some pain in her arm and asked the nurse what was causing it.

'Oh,' she replied, 'I had to give you both a painkilling injection.' Then, realising that she had carelessly left the vaccine bottle lying by the bed, she quickly snatched it up and put it in her pocket. Angela didn't have time to notice the words 'DECEPTION DRUG' written on the label.

She jumped up and found it strange as she looked around that the so-called hospital ward had only two beds and a nurse. The rest of the room was just windows and white walls. There was no medical equipment, no stethoscopes or trollies—in fact nothing—not even a clock or a calendar. But she didn't comment and went to the door. 'Thanks. Oh, Nurse, if yer'll excuse me, I think I'll just go and find me—ah—boyfriend.'

As she walked outside, she noticed that the sun had gone in and dusk had fallen, but what she couldn't tell was how long she had actually been there. She entered a large building that reminded her of an ancient museum and was shocked when she found out it was. The enormous hall was packed with everything from skeletons of prehistoric monsters to the first spaceship that took a man to the planet Mercury. There were spears and guns, chariots and racing cars, scrolls and computer screens, even ancient coins and credit cards. It seemed like all of history was housed here.

'Little Christian,' she yelled, and her voice echoed all around the large building.

'Over here, Angela,' came a reply. 'In between the carpenter's shop and the chocolate factory.' The building was so enormous that it took Angela another fifteen minutes to locate Little Christian.

He looked very busy. 'I thought you were never coming,' he joked. Angela stared at him. He looked so different—a pencil behind one ear, his hair grown long. He was wearing spectacles and also looked very pale and thin.

'How long 'ave we bin 'ere?' she enquired.

'I haven't got a clue,' shrugged Little Christian. 'Hours, days, weeks, months, maybe years. Who cares? This place is the place of my dreams and I am happy to stay here for ever.'

Angela's head was starting to hurt. 'Yeah,' she said, 'but I'm sure we woz goin' somewhere important before we came 'ere.'

'Rubbish,' chuckled Little Christian. 'There is nowhere as important as here.'

Angela's head was now pounding. Her mind was fighting the drug that she had been given. 'Yeah, but wot about— wot about—wot about—wot was 'is name?' Her head now screamed with pain. 'Yeah, wot about ... the Voice?'

Little Christian pushed his glasses up onto the top of his head. 'Angela,' he said in a very condescending tone, 'that is what I am studying here—the history of the Manual and how we got to be where we are today. You cannot believe how helpful it's been. I feel like a new man with fascinating, fresh insights. Look, come with me and let me point out a few facts to you. Stop thinking—you're giving yourself a headache.

'Now what do you think they are?' he asked, pointing to a large, beautiful garden with two stuffed animals in it.

'They're monkeys,' Angela replied.

'Now that is where you are wrong! They are Newchurch's ancestors, Adam and Eve.'

'But they're not people, they're monkeys,' argued Angela.

'Listen, Angela, you must be open to learn. What I am discovering here is that the Voice never really created anything. For instance, did you know that billions of years ago a blob came from nowhere and everything evolved from that blob? First the blob became a jellyfish, the jellyfish became a pig, the pig became a monkey and the monkey became a human being.'

'Don't that sound a bit far-fetched?' asked Angela. 'Yer'd need a lot of faith ta believe that.'

'No, faith has got nothing to do with it,' continued Little Christian. 'It's a proven fact. An intelligent ex-monkey called Darly Charwin said so. Look, I've been studying here for ages while you have been asleep, and it seems to me that neither the Voice nor the Manual are all they are cracked up to be. Listen, let me show you two more things that actually prove that the Voice was just another human being like us. What do you think that is?' He pointed to a picture frame on the wall.

'It's a very old photo of a mum, a dad and a tiny baby.'

'Yes, that's right, an ordinary mum and dad with an ordinary baby. Read that little plaque next to it.'

Angela read it out loud. "'Ere is a picture of the Voice wiv 'is mum and dad. In the twentief century a bishop from Oldchurch proved wivout a shadow of doubt that there woz nofin' unusual or supernatural about the Voice's conception or parenthood. 'E was just a cute little baby wiv ordinary parents."

'Wow!' said Angela. 'But 'ow did 'e prove it?'

'I don't know,' said Little Christian, getting a little irritated. 'All I know is that these people are more clever than you or I will ever be, so they must be right. I mean no one threw the bishop out of Oldchurch for being a heretic, did they? So presumably all of Oldchurch must have agreed with what he taught.

'And what about this?' he went on, pulling her along to the far corner of the room. 'Look at that, a replica of the cross and the tomb. But according to scientific research the Voice never really died on the cross; he only fainted. Then when he was buried he got his strength back and then appeared to people pretending to have risen from the dead. Now read that board there,' he continued.

Angela read in big bold letters the words: 'MEDICAL

RESEARCH CATEGORICALLY STATES THAT THERE IS NO SUCH THING AS RESURRECTION FROM THE DEAD.'

Little Christian stood back and started rubbing his arm.

'Wot's the trouble?' asked Angela.

'Well, Nurse Itbetter has to inject us each day to keep us healthy, and it must be due soon because I am starting to feel a bit strange.'

Sure enough, he had hardly finished his sentence when he heard the door of the building open and close and the clump of her shoes on the marble floor heading towards them.

'Little Christian, supposin' all that yer've learned is true, can ya answer me two questions? The first is wot use will it be even if ya fill all yer 'ead wiv all this knowledge if ya spend the rest of yer life in this 'ere quarry and secondly why—if ye'r learning so much vital information—are ya lookin' so thin and ill? At least the Voice seemed ta look after ya.'

Before he could answer the questions the nurse had arrived and asked them to roll up their sleeves. As he lifted his arm up he accidentally jogged the nurse and the vaccine bottle went flying through the air and smashed on the hard floor.

'I'm ever so sorry, Nurse,' said Little Christian.

'Oh, never mind,' said the nurse. 'I've plenty more where that came from. Get on with your studying and I'll just go and get another one.'

As the nurse left, Angela noticed the white wet label lying in the vaccine. 'I wonder wot painkiller she's givin' us?' she said, picking it up. 'Oh no!' she gasped. 'Little Christian, read this!'

'DECEPTION DRUG ... what does that mean?' he said.

'It means all this in 'ere is a pack of lies and a trick of the Enemy Superpowers to try and make us turn against the

Voice.' She was beginning to sense the effects of the drug wearing off.

Little Christian was still under the influence of the drug. Along with the hours of lies he had been studying, it had taken its toll and numbed his once sharp mind.

Angela had to act quickly. 'Please, Voice, what do we do now?' she cried.

The Voice turned her head around and she saw a display of an altar drenched with water. By the side of it stood an old prophet who according to the Manual called down fire from heaven to prove the existence of the Voice. A table next to it contained a matchbox and a plaque which said, 'It was not possible for the Voice to send down fire from heaven, and it has been proved without any doubt that the prophet had a packet of these burnwater matches in his back pocket.'

Angela grabbed the matches, struck one and threw it on the altar. Immediately all the relics started to burn with amazing speed. She pulled Little Christian out of the door. The combination of the smell of smoke, the fresh air and the drug wearing off at last started bringing him back to his senses.

They ran as fast as they could and started to scramble up the quarry face. Although it was fairly steep there were plenty of footholds and handholds. It was like someone had gone before them and prepared it for them.

As they were nearing the top they heard a voice boom out, 'Where do you think you are going?' Little Christian would have recognised that voice anywhere and turning around he saw the enormous body of Greedy Gutrot standing next to his evil mausoleum.

As Gutrot stood shouting and cursing, unaware that the mausoleum was on fire, he didn't notice that the fire had also started burning the bottom of his clothes. (Of course he couldn't have noticed this as his massive belly obscured his view!) It wasn't until he felt himself burning that he realised he was part of what was now an unquenchable blaze.

Little Christian and Angela reached the safety of the top just in time to see Gutrot and his evil creation melt into a gooey mess. 'That's the end of 'im,' cheered Angela.

'I'm afraid not,' said Little Christian. 'He will keep coming back until the day when the Voice finishes him off for good.'

Once back on the main path again they noticed a pretty little building called Restoration Cottage by the side of the road. It was all painted white and had the most beautiful sweet-smelling flowers growing all around it.

Little Christian opened his photomap. 'Hey, guess what?' he cheered. 'This belongs to the Voice. It's on the photomap. Let's stay here for a while as I must spend some time talking to him and also reading my Manual to get rid of all those evil lies that I have allowed to enter my brain.'

'Good idea,' said Angela, 'but first follow me.' She went into the cottage and on finding the kitchen she sat him down on a chair while she went rummaging through some kitchen drawers. 'Got 'em!' she yelled triumphantly, then seeing he was still wearing his spectacles took them off and threw them into the rubbish bin. 'Ya don't really want to keep any of Greedy Gutrot's souveniers, do ya?' she chuckled. Then she pulled out from behind her back a shiny pair of scissors. 'And now for the hair.'

Little Christian gulped and hoped that he wouldn't end up like Samson.

Over the next few days he spent hours with the Manual. He read how he was made as a man in the Voice's image. He was pleased that he had never been a blob or a monkey. He also rediscovered about the Voice's miraculous conception to an ordinary woman—hardly more than a Littlekid herself, how his only Father was the one in heaven and finally how he was beaten up and killed, even had a spear pushed into his flesh to make sure that he was dead. And then after three days he came back to life again. 'How could I ever have believed those lies?' he thought. 'After all, if there had not been a resurrection there would be no Children of the Voice.'

9
Robots Rule OK

Professor Mindwarpt couldn't help himself laughing out loud as he saw Harmony, weeping and confused, staggering over the rough rocks of the Bigwideworld but not having a clue about where she was going. 'Good,' he thought, rubbing his hands together in glee, 'another possible danger source I can cross off my list.'

Although he was reasonably happy with all the progress, he was also very angry that Heavy Shepherd and Lucy Morals had nearly blown the whole lot through some stupid lovey-doveyness—and worse still allowed a Littlekid on a skateboard to spy on them. 'When I've finished this assignment I will reprogram that pair of love-struck lily-livered lugbrains to be a couple of TV gameshow hosts. That will bring them down to earth!' He grinned.

His other worry was that none of his evil superbreeds seemed to be having any influence over the smaller Littlekids. It was as if they recognised the infiltrators, whereas the older ones didn't seem to notice.

He then opened two more of his coffins. 'Now for two nice ordinary superbreeds,' he muttered. 'We have enough at leadership level. Now it's time to hit grass roots!'

The first of his superbreeds to step out was a loud-mouthed, simple character who was very theatrical and couldn't stop talking. He rarely thought—he just spoke. He was of medium build, wore a blue pinstripe suit and smart spectacles.

'Welcome, Namit Claimit,' said Mindwarpt. 'You should not only add a bit of yuppieness to Newchurch, but should also ensure that any faith in the Voice's supernatural power that may still be lurking around will soon evaporate.'

The second Littlekid was a young lady called Tiff Withallsorts—an ordinary Littlekid who would never stand out in a crowd. In fact, you would hardly notice she was there. Average size, average build, in fact the word 'average' would just about sum her up.

'Now, Tiff,' said Mindwarpt, 'I don't suppose I need to remind you that you need to be friends with all those who are discontented, and stir them up in everything. I even give you permission to stir things up against Heavy. After all, he's big enough and ugly enough to take care of himself,' he snarled.

Mindwarpt gave them the usual warning about if they were disobedient he would terminate them. Then after they had both said, 'Yes, O Mighty Supervoice,' he let them drift off to infiltrate Newchurch.

Rhoda sat prisoner, locked in a bedroom in Lucy Morals' and Dodgy Prophet's house. All she had left in the world was a skateboard and she couldn't even use that in this tiny room. It must have been a week since she had spoken to anyone, and she was really missing her friend Harmony. Although she was very frightened about what was happening in Newchurch she knew that she must escape and try to do something to help.

She'd already tried the windows and doors a number of times but there was no way she would get out through these. Then she had an idea. Once a day Lucy brought her some bread and water—opened the door, put them on a table, then walked out. This would be her only chance of escape.

While Rhoda was working out her plan, other very important plans were being discussed by all the members of Newchurch. Heavy stood up at the front, accompanied by Dodgy Prophet and Lucy Morals, and told all the people that he had some very exciting improvements and announcements to make. 'Amen,' said Dodgy, having already seen the proposals.

'First, we are changing the name of Newchurch.' The people gasped and whispered among themselves. 'Now don't look so surprised,' he continued. 'Two things I have always maintained is that we must not get stuck in a rut and we must learn to honour those in leadership over us.'

'Amen,' shouted Dodgy again.

'So we shall henceforth be known as the Newagechurch of the Heavy Shepherd.

While the adults sat too frightened to move, a few of the Littlekids walked out in disgust.

'Secondly, we are all very sorry to hear that Buddy has had some sort of breakdown, so we feel it right to take him off the leadership for the time being for his own good. Obviously the strain of leadership was too much for him.'

The adults remembered what it was like when Little Christian, Angela and Harmony were around and sat thinking about it. The Littlekids also remembered those days, and more left the meeting.

'Thirdly, first the bad news: Dodgy Prophet confided in me today that he and Lucy are, sadly, to be divorced. Of course they still have a great respect for each other, but as so often happens, they have found they are incompatible. Still, all is not lost because the good news is that Lucy has agreed to be my bride and Dodgy has agreed to be my best man.' Lucy smiled and Dodgy refrained from saying amen. The remainder of the Littlekids left the building.

'And, finally, our younger Littlekids are all getting a bit out of hand and rebellious, so I've decided that they will not be meeting with us adults any longer. "Family" is a word of the past anyway. I believe that the Voice has no time for these younger Littlekids—they just get in his way and ours. He is really only interested in us older ones. Lucy and I will take over the running of the Littlekids' meeting. We believe that there is a lot they can learn from us. We will have our first meeting tomorrow night in our ... I mean Lucy's house.' Of course, no littlekids were around to hear this statement.

As Heavy sat down, Dodgy stood up. 'Adults and Littlekids of the Newagechurch of the Heavy Shepherd: I believe you would want to join me in honouring our devoted leader and his new bride by a gift. I suggest that we build them a house, a nice brand new two-bedroomed bungalow.'

'Rubbish,' shouted a voice in the congregation.

Heavy leaped up with a red face, ready to take some heavy authority, but Dodgy kept in firm control. 'Who said that?' he shouted.

'I did,' said a stranger walking to the front.

'Who on earth are you?' said Dodgy and Heavy together. 'We've never seen you before.'

'My name is Namit Claimit,' he shouted, standing at the front. 'And I think that it's a disgrace. If our leader is half as good as you say he is, then he and his new bride should have a *twenty*-bedroomed mansion, with an indoor swimming pool, colour televisions and a jaccuzi in every room, including the kitchen.'

Heavy looked stunned. Dodgy looked embarrassed, and Lucy looked thrilled. Everyone else looked towards the door. 'Of course it's right, what you are saying,' said Dodgy, 'but I'm not sure we've got that sort of money.'

Namit looked at the people. 'Hands up all those who believe that nothing is too hard for the Voice.' Everyone's hand went up. 'Right,' he said. 'Now hands up all those who believe that the Voice loves his children and wants to give them the best.'

Again all hands went up.

'Well, come on, Children of the Voice, let's not only believe for it, but let's name it before each other, then claim it from the Voice. After all, the Voice is no man's debtor.'

Everyone followed Namit's instructions.

'Now,' continued Dodgy, 'I believe that faith without works is dead, as the Manual says. So I suggest that on Friday night when you all get your paypackets, you bring them unopened into the office. Here we will open them for you and put nine-tenths of the money into the mansion fund and give you back a tenth.'

'Brilliant,' said Namit Claimit. 'Amazing, faith-building incentive. If you don't feel that you can live on the tenth, name the amount of money you need, then claim it from the Voice. Remember, his resources are unlimited and this is a surefire way to make the Children of the Voice children of mighty faith.'

The meeting closed, but everyone was asked to stay for an

hour to thank the Voice for the opportunity that had been entrusted to them to provide for his work.

Unbeknown to the leaders, however, a note was being passed around the hall advertising a special meeting that had been secretly arranged for all those who were fed up with Heavy Shepherd's dictatorship. The meeting would be held in the home of a new member, Tiff Withallsorts.

While people were praying, Lucy slipped out of the side door and ran home, remembering that it was time to feed Rhoda. She was very excited at the prospect of the forthcoming marriage and even more about the forthcoming mansion; she didn't really have her mind on what she was doing. She put Rhoda's bread and water on a tray and whistled away happily to herself as she climbed the stairs.

This was Rhoda's big night, maybe her last chance to escape. The bedroom was dark as she had closed the curtains and was lying in wait behind the cupboard. She heard footsteps coming up the stairs; the lock clicked, then the bedroom door opened.

In the gloom and half-light Lucy didn't realise that she had put her right foot onto a skateboard. The minute the foot made contact, the skateboard took off, taking the screaming Lucy with it. The tray with the bread and water was thrown into the air while the skateboard stopped abruptly at the wall. Lucy, however, did not stop. The skateboard had stopped directly below the window and she continued on, flying head-first straight through it.

Rhoda leaped out from behind the cupboard, screaming as she heard the glass shatter. 'What have I done?' she yelled, not daring to look out of the window, frightened at what she might see. Rhoda grabbed her skateboard, rushed downstairs and ran for her life through the back door.

On the concrete underneath the window lay Lucy Morals. Not dead or lying in a pool of blood as Rhoda would have expected to see ... but disassembled with wires hanging out and sparks flying everywhere.

The Littlekids who had left the meeting early stood gazing at the sizzling remains of the electronic Lucy and realised for the first time that their enemies were not flesh and blood. They'd seen too much. From now on life would be dangerous for them. They must go into hiding; they must take Newchurch underground.

10

Deadbody

Professor Mindwarpt, who was usually so observant, was in his hideout overlooking Newchurch; but he failed to notice a frightened little girl carrying a skateboard run past him. He was far too busy trying to work out why one of his superbreeds had ceased to function.

Back at Newchurch a heartbroken Heavy Shepherd had found the remains of Lucy—fortunately before any of the adults had seen her. Quickly he had gathered her up in a sack and hidden her in a shed around the back of his house with the intention of taking her back to the Professor to see if she could be repaired. As he hid her, thinking his secret was safe, he failed to see that dozens of little eyes were watching his every move.

These same little eyes had found sanctuary in the cellar underneath the meeting hall. They spent the days reading their Manuals, spying on the invaders and praying to the Voice that Little Christian would return.

On seeing that Rhoda Skateboard had escaped and was obviously the cause of the demise of his beloved, he immediately circulated a news letter to all members explaining that Rhoda had not only gone missing, but she had also become violent and totally uncontrollable. In his opinion she had allowed an Enemy Superpower to come in and control her life.

'If anyone sees her or hears of her whereabouts, he should not approach her. She is dangerous. He must contact Heavy Shepherd immediately who, along with some experienced helpers, will give her the attention she requires. This is for her own good.'

Heavy also went on to say that no younger Littlekids had turned up to his meeting: 'Rumour has it that they have vanished. If any of these younger Littlekids are caught, they must be brought directly to me, so that I can serve them the appropriate punishment for rebellion.'

With no mention of Lucy, the letter finished.

Little Christian and Angela felt fully refreshed and restored as they entered the gates of Deadbody. It was a strange sort of place, reminiscent of Oldchurch yet with many different features. The strangest thing was that all the adults and Littlekids had smiles on their faces which were just like masks. They were obviously not happy, yet these grins tried to put over the impression that they were. They also either wore bright red clothes or dull grey ones.

Another unusual feature was that their skin was white. In fact they really did look like walking corpses with happy faces. Angela leaned over and whispered that a few days ago she had thought that Little Christian had looked unhealthy, but she was very thankful that he had never looked like these people ... though she would have loved to see Little Christian in one of the trendy red outfits.

In spite of all their strange features, the occupants of Deadbody did seem to be caring people, especially those dressed in red. One lady in red, called Mrs Ownway, beckoned them over to her house and invited them in for a cup of tea. As they entered Chalk and Cheese Cottage and sat down she pointed over to her husband who was seated with his head buried in a book and apologised that he was a grey. Her husband just grunted with a smile.

Little Christian and Angela glanced around the room and were not surprised that all its contents were either grey or red depending on whether they belonged to the husband or the wife.

Mrs Ownway explained that they had a couple of spare bedrooms and offered to put up Little Christian and Angela up for the night, apologising that the colour of the rooms might not be to their liking. But Little Christian and Angela explained that they had no preference between red and grey. Both the husband and wife look shocked.

After a short chat both the Ownways got up and explained that it was time for their meeting. Little Christian and Angela said that they would go with them.

The church building was only a short walk away from the house. Little Christian was interested to note that the outside of the building looked absolutely awful. It was like two opposing building companies had started building from different ends and had used different plans. It was also a mixture of the grey stones from Oldchurch and the new, bright-red bricks he associated with Newchurch.

As they walked through the large doors he was again stunned by what he saw. To start with all the reds gave each other a welcoming hug, while the greys stood their distance and firmly shook each other by the hand. Little Christian and Angela, being visitors, both got a hug and a handshake each.

Then all the people in red were handed just the new half of the Manual, a songsheet and a tambourine. They all sat down on modern red plastic chairs on the left side of the building. All the people in grey, however, were handed just the old half of the Manual, an ancient hymnbook and a candle and they all sat on hard wooden benches on the right side.

Little Christian and Angela, being visitors, were handed both halves of the Manual, a songsheet and a hymnbook, plus of course the tambourine and the candle. They needed a shopping trolley to carry it all! They decided after a lot of thought to sit on the red chairs, purely because they looked more comfortable.

At the front of the building on the left side, facing them, stood a rock band dressed in red. They had a large public address system, an electronic drum kit, a stack of keyboards, lead and bass guitars, plus a whole brass section. By contrast, on the right at the front was a massive old wind organ with enormous great metal pipes stretching to the ceiling.

As things were about to start, two doors opened—one on the left and one on the right. Out walked seven leaders in red and seven leaders in grey who sat in their appropriate places facing their appropriate people. Then, from a door in the middle, a man who was obviously the chief leader entered wearing a suit that was exactly divided: fifty per cent red down one side and fifty per cent grey down the other. He even wore one red sock and shoe and one grey sock and shoe. Around his neck he had a whistle and in his hands a stop-watch and a notebook.

'Wot on earth 'ave we come to 'ere?' whispered Angela.

'That's our full-time ref,' explained a helpful red lady sitting next to her, who had to Angela's embarrassment overheard her whisper.

All went silent as a red and a grey leader rose together. The grey leader was the first to speak, 'We will begin to give thanks to the Voice by singing hymn number 301.'

'Excuse me,' said the red leader, still smiling of course, 'I do believe that it is our turn to begin this morning.' Then turning to the people in red he announced that they would begin to celebrate the Voice with song number 3 on their songsheets.

'I'm sorry,' said the leader in grey before a note had been struck, 'but you are offside.'

The whistle blew and, taking a coin from his pocket, the ref asked the grey leader to call heads or tails. The greys won. 'Greys start with hymn number 301. This will immediately be followed by the reds' song number 3.'

The mighty organ pounded out the music as the greys stood as upright and still as statues singing the words of their favourite hymn 'The Voice of old is the Voice we love'. The reds ignored them, while some even yawned.

The minute they finished and sat down, the red musicians' amplifiers were switched on. With the accompanying shriek of feedback, the chairs were pushed back and those dressed in red started to leap around bashing tambourines. Everything was at full volume as they too sang one of their favourite songs:

Hallelujah, Voice,
Hallelujah, Voice,
Voice Hallelujah,
Hallelujah, Voice.

Although the whole song was only made up of two words, they still managed to make it last twice as long as the greys' hymn. During this time the greys shook their heads and put their fingers in their ears.

As they sat down Angela and Little Christian looked at each other in disgust. 'This is terrible,' they both whispered at the same time.

The ref stood up and announced that due to the length of the reds' song, the greys now had five minutes' penalty time added on. 'It is now time for prayers,' announced the ref, looking at his notebook. 'Greys to start.'

Then the greys reopened their hymnbooks and read out some of the hymns, this time as prayers. The reds muttered 'religious' and 'contrived' under their breaths.

Then came the reds' turn. They all stood up and started speaking in what they claimed to be the Voice's special language, which of course no one understood—not even the Voice. The greys just stared at them as though they had one sandwich short in their picnic baskets.

At the end the ref stood up and holding up a yellow card told the reds that this was their first official public warning. Once again they had gone into overtime and it was his job to see that both sides prayed fairly. He also knew that later on in the meeting the reds would try and take a further unfair advantage with a healing session; they would be sure to take that into injury time.

The two preachers were about to begin. Just as the grey Littlekids who were forced to go out were preparing to go to their babysitters and the red Littlekids who were forced to stay in were climbing into their sleeping bags on the floor—Little Christian could suffer no more.

'Wait!' he yelled, walking to the front. 'I've come to bring you word from the Voice.'

The red leaders and the grey leaders stared at each other, still smiling of course, each thinking that the other was trying to gain an unfair advantage by bringing on a substitute.

'OK, Littlekid,' said the ref, 'but you will first have to tell me whose side you are on so that I can allow extra time to the others.'

'I'm on the Voice's side,' shouted Little Christian.

'Yes, and so are we,' said the reds and the greys spontaneously together.

'No, you're not. Neither of you are,' screamed back Little Christian. 'Will you please listen to me just for a few minutes? Then I will explain.'

'OK,' said the ref stopping his watch. 'I'll count this as half-time.'

Little Christian turned and looked at the ref. 'Why is he smiling all the time?' he asked. 'And why are you smiling all the time?' he said, pointing at the people.'

'Because we are happy,' they all shouted back.

'No you're not,' argued Little Christian, 'you're just pretending, you're being unreal.'

'Go on. Sock it to 'em,' yelled a loyal supporter from the back, and Little Christian guessed who that was.

'That's a great idea, Angela,' he shouted back. 'Watch this, everyone,' and turning around he whacked the ref in the face. The people gasped, but then they saw the ref's face start to crack. The smiling mask fell to pieces and smashed on the floor like china. And there looking at everyone was a ref with a very sad real face.

'Now, the rest of you. I dare you to have the courage to face up to what you are really like,' shouted Little Christian. 'Go on—if you really care for the person sitting next to you, smack him or her in the face.'

Everyone hesitated for a minute, then, as the red and grey leaders walked over and started smacking each other, everyone else joined in. Masks shattered, cracked and splintered to the floor all around the building. In no time at all, a large number of sad real people sat facing the front.

Little Christian walked over to one of the grey leaders and asked him why he was there.

'We greys have been here since the beginning. This is our building. Even the walls were a revered grey to start with until the reds built on their obscene brick extensions. We enjoy worshipping the Voice in our own old-fashioned way, and we refuse to let the reds take us over with their fancy gimmicks.'

Little Christian walked over to a red leader and asked him why he was there. 'This is where the Voice has called us to be. We are here to bring change and new vision to the greys. We don't like it here and get very little from the meetings, but that's not the point. We must stay here and annoy the greys till the Voice tells us it's time to move on.'

Little Christian walked up to the ref, 'Why are you here?' he enquired.

The ref looked at him sadly. 'Many years ago I came to teach folk more about the Voice and the Manual, but that never came about. With two opposing stubborn teams both claiming to be right, it's been more than a full-time job just to keep the peace. I do wonder how much longer I can carry on in the middle though. It really takes it out of me, and my health and friendship with the Voice are suffering.'

'Good news! The Voice has an answer for all of you if you are willing to listen,' said Little Christian, turning back to face the people. 'My friend Angela is one of the Voice's directors, and I believe the Voice has already been speaking to her so that she can come and give you a solution to this terrible mess.'

Angela walked to the front with one hand covering her face. 'Are you all right,' enquired Little Christian, wondering if she was still praying.

'Of course I am, ya nitwit,' whispered Angela. 'It's just that thanks to yer hair-brained scheme of everyone slappin' each other's chops, one over-enthusiastic red slapped mine, but as ya well know I'm not wearin' a mask to protect me.' She pulled her hand down to reveal a lovely black eye. Little Christian couldn't help smiling. 'I'll sort ya out later,' she said, deliberately standing on his toe.

Fortunately, Angela's whack on the face had not stopped her from hearing what the Voice wanted to say. She explained that it was right that the greys should be allowed to continue to worship the Voice in this building in their own way. She suggested that the Voice had not told the reds to stay here and be disgruntled. In fact they were deceived and actually restricting the Voice's plans. The Voice was not interested in where people worshipped, she said, but he was concerned that they did worship and were happy and real people who honoured and loved their leaders. Angela suggested that the reds should meet in their local school hall as from next week as it would be much more appropriate for what they wanted to do.

'But that will destroy our unity,' said the ref.

Little Christian butted in, 'What unity? Sadly, at this stage there is no unity, and to keep up this pretence will never materialise. Unity will come as people live for the Voice, learn to respect those who may differ from them in certain things, but also are part of a church in which they feel secure and at home. Believe it or not,' Little Christian went on, 'to seperate will actually bring you closer together. If you allow personal conflict and competition to be a thing of the past, you can then really unite in a plan that is going to help the real needy, those lost out there in the Bigwideworld.'

Angela was looking at the ref. 'Drop the name "ref." Ya dont need it any longer. The Voice tells me that there is a place waitin' for ya at the Trainin' Module if ya want it. Ye'r damaged, and ya need a few repairs.'

Immediately the ex-ref jumped up and without needing

to be told twice ran out of the door. Both Little Christian and Angela guessed that he probably wouldn't stop running until he reached the Training Module.

Both the red and grey leaders could see the sense in what Little Christian and Angela had said, and would give the seperate meetings and the unity a try. With that, the building emptied.

Later, Little Christian and Angela sat exhausted in the living room of Chalk and Cheese Cottage too tired even to talk. Angela had a steak over her bruised eye while Little Christian just lay back in his chair sniffing the paint fumes; their hosts were racing around the house painting everything ... green!

II

The Last Resort

'Psst.'

The Littlekid jumped. 'Who's there?' she cried, staring at a large thick bush in front of her.

'Are you by yourself?' the voice continued.

'Yes,' said the Littlekid, 'but who are you?'

The bush swept to one side as Harmony came out from behind it.

'Harmony!' shouted Rhoda, running up and giving her a hug. 'I thought I would never see you again.'

The two girls sat down and Rhoda related all the latest news from Newchurch. After Rhoda had finished sobbing and talking, Harmony stood up and declared that if Heavy and his evil mob wanted a war, she was prepared to give him one.

'Oh, I've never heard you speak like this before,' exclaimed Rhoda. 'I'm frightened. After all, these are very dangerous people we are going to be fighting against.'

'That's true,' said Harmony. 'But what is the difference between us and them?'

Rhoda thought for a moment then with a big beam on her face said, 'I know—we have the Voice on our side.'

'Yes, and nobody is more powerful than he is. What we are going to do now is spend some time talking to the Voice. Then we will go out and find some recruits to help us. Heavy Shepherd ... your days are numbered.'

'Yeah!' shouted Rhoda excitedly as they knelt down to talk to the Voice.

As darkness was closing in, a large figure crept out of the back door of his house and undid his shed door. He put a sack over his shoulder and, making sure that no one was following him, crept through Newchurch and made his way into the Bigwideworld.

Once a safe distance away he started whispering, 'O Mighty Supervoice, O Mighty Supervoice.'

'What are you doing here?' came a gruff reply from behind a rock. Out stepped Professor Mindwarpt who stared at Heavy Shepherd. 'Did I give you permission to come and find me?' he yelled angrily. 'You are made to obey, not take your own initiative.'

'Yes, but this is different, O Mighty Supervoice,' said Heavy, grovelling at his feet. 'This is a matter of life and death.'

'Well it certainly is,' said Mindwarpt, 'and it will probably be a matter of your life and death.'

Heavy got up and pointed to the sack. 'Please, O Mighty Supervoice, can I show you what's in here?'

'Oh, for goodness sake get on with it! The sooner you do, the sooner you can get back to where you should be.'

Heavy opened the sack, tipped the contents out in front of the Professor, then jumped back in amazement.

'Very interesting,' said Mindwarpt. 'But I have seen a pile of bricks before.'

'What has happened to my Lucy?' wailed Heavy. 'I put her in this sack after she fell through a window and went out of action, and I was hoping that you would repair her, O Mighty Supervoice.' Heavy began to blub.

'Now this is serious,' said Mindwarpt, stroking his chin thoughtfully. 'Lucy's termination is of no concern to me, but I thought that like a normal person you would have buried her and no one would have known that she wasn't a normal Littlekid. But now someone has her remains and realises that an invasion has taken place.' The Professor then turned and walked away from Heavy Shepherd. 'Wait here,' he ordered.

A few minutes later he came back with what was the last of his superbreeds. Heavy looked at the Littlekid facing him and stepped back in fear. This Littlekid had a face with no emotion and eyes that were as cold as ice. His body was bulging with muscle and he looked like he had the strength of at least ten normal Littlekids. He was the meanest, nastiest Littlekid imaginable.

'Heavy Shepherd, meet Percy ... Percy Cutor. From now on, Heavy, this is your right-hand man. I don't want any more democratic meetings. I don't want anyone else getting in my way, and Percy will help you achieve this. Percy, your first task is to find who has got the remains of Lucy and then you must not only eliminate that person, but see that there is no trace left of Lucy's remains, either.'

Heavy winced at the thought.

'Now move along, you two, time is running out and we have just been given a new assignment in a place called Deadbody, starting in a couple of weeks' time.'

Little Christian and Angela left Deadbody, their Commission completed. They hoped their work had been successful, but really now it was up to the people to act on what they had heard.

'It would 'ave bin so much easier if we could 'ave forced 'em ta listen to the Voice,' commented Angela.

'Yeah, you're right,' replied Little Christian. 'But you know as well as I do that the Voice does not force us to do things. He wants us to obey him because we love him.'

'Yeah,' agreed Angela. 'I know that, but it still would 'ave bin a whole lot easier.' She grabbed hold of Little Christian's hand. 'Well, wot do ya really fink of me?' she asked boldly.

'Um,' said Little Christian carefully, 'I suppose I quite like you really.'

'Is that all?' said Angela, smiling. 'Don't ya love me and fink that we make a good team and might 'ave a future togever?' she continued.

'I'll let you know when we are back in the safety of Newchurch,' laughed Little Christian.

'Promise?' said Angela.

'Yeah, I promise,' said Little Christian. 'I can't wait to get back to see all our friends in Newchurch,' he continued, changing the subject. 'And according to the photomap there is a short-cut, so it shouldn't take us long to get there.'

'That's great,' said Angela. 'It's like the Voice wants us to get back quickly. Perhaps they are missing us.'

'I'm sure they are,' replied little Christian.

'I don't like it here much,' whispered Rhoda. 'It's lonely and creepy, all dark and misty. I can't see anything that is living anywhere. It's all just like a big slag heap, and all these tombstones everywhere really give me the creeps. What are we here for, Harmony?'

'Well, Rhoda, this is the place people come to when they feel fed up with life and cannot see any point in living. This really is their last resort. If you keep walking for a few more kilometres you come to a big screen that hangs down from the sky called the final curtain. Once you go through that screen you never come back.'

'Well, that's cheered me up,' said Rhoda. 'But surely things haven't got that bad for us?'

Harmony smiled. 'No, and they never will for Children of the Voice. But I have a friend who is always hanging around here hoping to rescue people and stop them before they reach the final curtain.'

Then suddenly they heard a voice shouting out from quite a distance in front of them. 'Turn back from the final curtain. Believe in the Voice, then leave this death and darkness and experience light and life!'

'Ah, that sounds like just the person we are looking for. Is that you, Hearthunter?' shouted Harmony.

A figure seemed to come rushing out of nowhere towards them and gave both the girls a hug. 'Wow! It's great to see a friendly face,' he exclaimed. 'I've had one of those days when no one seems to listen to me. In fact they just ignore me.'

Harmony explained that she knew how he felt, but that she had some very important news to share with him regarding Newchurch. She wondered if he could spare the time to listen, then maybe to help them.

'No sweat,' he said. 'I've loads of my mates patrolling this patch twenty-four hours a day; they'll cover for me. Follow me and I'll take you out of this doom and gloom. Then you can tell me what the problem is.'

Hearthunter heard the tragic news, and tears came into his eyes. 'But we thought that Newchurch was invincible. We were convinced that we were strong and could never get into these sorts of problems. Maybe we were a bit too proud and complacent.'

'It would be good if we could find Miraclekid on the way back. We may need his gifts to sort these Littlekids out.'

'How will we find him?' asked Rhoda.

'Well, that's the problem,' said Hearthunter. 'Nobody ever finds Miraclekid. He finds you. By the way, does Little Christian know all about what's been going on?'

'I don't think he does,' replied Harmony.

'Well, when's he due back there?' asked Hearthunter.

'Again, I'm not sure,' said Harmony, 'but it must be any day now.'

'We'd better move quickly,' Hearthunter then continued. 'If Little Christian arrives back before us unaware of what has happened, he won't have a chance, He must be at the top of their hitlist!'

12

Faults in the Foundations

Tiff Withallsorts was achieving wonders. She had different groups meeting in her home every day and called her meetings 'The Back to the Voice Group'. It was thrilling for her to see that more and more people were becoming negative and critical.

She convinced one group that the name 'The Newage-church of the Heavy Shepherd' was far too long and thought that they should abbreviate it to just 'Newage-church'. After she had persuaded them all to agree, she then asked them what was the matter with the name 'Newagechurch' and in no time they were all arguing with each other again about what it should be called.

As Heavy's mansion was beginning to be built she asked an interior design group to discuss the interior. Again, within an hour, they were all at each other's throats, all of them thinking that their own ideas were the best.

She also started a men's group and began the meeting by congratulating them on their giving towards the project, but then managed to persuade them to say what they were earning. She enquired if it was fair that some were earning more than others and some were giving more than others. Yet again voices were raised as jealousy and anger reigned.

Namit Claimit had become a firm favourite with the Children of the Voice and had started his own Faithschool. So far there had been only two minor disasters. The first was when he encouraged his schoolchildren to jump off the hospital roof, claiming that the Voice would catch them before they reached the ground. Unfortunately, as the first person jumped, the Voice decided not to catch him. The rest came down and visited their friend inside the hospital, where he now lay wrapped up in bandages.

The second occasion was when he had a family faith-building session and he decided to pass around a very large snake and said that they must not be afraid to handle it. The faith level immediately shot up when he explained that the snake was not poisonous, but sank rapidly when the enormous snake decided to swallow one of the Littlekids.

Percy Cutor had been very quiet and laid-back since he arrived. He just seemed to watch and listen and take everything in. Heavy and Dodgy didn't trust him, mainly because he was so quiet and they were not. Lucy's remains and the younger Littlekids had still not been found and everyone, especially the men, were beginning to ask where Lucy was. Heavy sent out a special news letter saying that she had just gone away for a short while to see her parents and to tell them about the good news of her marriage.

Buddy meanwhile continued to lie in the hospital ward. He was getting no better. In fact, he was growing weaker all the time.

The Professor sat in the sun enjoying the feeling of success. The Children of the Voice had already started leaving Newchurch and rushing back to the security and stability of another Oldchurch, full of repentance. He could almost hear them apologising that they hadn't listened to their elders when they had warned them that Littlekids could never run a church or be of any use to the Voice.

Just as he sat there dreaming, a big cloud blotted out the sun. He opened his eyes to see it wasn't in fact a cloud but a singed, charred fat man called Greedy Gutrot.

'Well done, Gutrot!' said the Professor, laughing at his hilarious choice of phrase.

'Listen here, you, no jokes!' screamed Gutrot. 'This is no laughing matter.'

'Oh forgive me, I am sorry, sir,' continued Mindwarpt, 'but there's no need to get all fired up!' And again he went into cackles of laughter until Gutrot trod on his special cage and crushed it.

'Now will you shut up?' he said.

The Professor was hurt about having his cage wrecked; but looking at the angry mountain standing next to him, he didn't feel that now was a wise time to tell him.

As Mindwarpt explained that Newchurch was nearly all over, Gutrot calmed down and sat alongside him. He made him repeat the story again and again as he so loved to hear it. And of course each time the Professor told the story he would add extra little bits to make his plots seem even more of an achievement.

After the fifth telling, Mindwarpt asked Gutrot how he had fared against Little Christian. Gutrot immediately started to get angry again as he recollected that he had almost had him. 'Thanks to some stupid girl, he got away.'

The Professor looked up with interest. 'A girl, you say? Can you describe this girl to me?'

'Well,' said Gutrot, 'she was an ordinary looking Littlekid in her early teens, I would guess. Obviously quite experienced in the Voice's service. Skinny—oh, yeah, I know—she spoke with a funny accent.'

Mindwarpt leaped to his feet. 'Angela!' he bellowed. 'You are describing Angela.'

'So what?' said Gutrot, amazed at how the Professor had suddenly become so incensed.

'One of my top superbreeds, Percy Cutor, had given her hours of special attention and put her through the most excrutiating torture that any Littlekid has ever experienced. I heard it with my own ears. How in the name of all that's evil did she manage to live?'

Gutrot and Mindwarpt were so wrapped up in their conversation that they failed to noticed two excited Littlekids walking by them with their arms around each other. They had been on a long journey, but they were now just minutes away from Newchurch.

13
Trash Metal

As Harmony, Rhoda and Hearthunter jogged along the path leading to Newchurch they suddenly heard the most awful noise they had ever heard coming from behind a large hill on their left.

'What's that?' asked Rhoda as they all ground to a halt.

Hearthunter's ears pricked up and suddenly his face grew very excited. 'Wow! If that's what I think it is, we must get over there straight away,' he said enthusiastically.

'Wait a minute,' replied Harmony, looking a little bit concerned. 'You yourself said it was urgent that we find

91

Miraclekid then rush back to Newchurch in case Little Christian and Angela beat us there.'

'Did I?' said Hearthunter with a deliberately forgetful memory. 'Yes I probably did,' he admitted, looking at the frown that had appeared on Rhoda's face. 'Even so,' he continued, 'I'm a Hearthunter and I must get my priorities right. Over that hill there are needy people who have never heard of the Voice. I mean, at least we know that the Voice will protect Little Christian and Angela.'

Neither Harmony nor Rhoda could argue with that. They also knew that when Hearthunter got even a sniff of a lost Littlekid, nothing would distract him until he had gone and shared the good news of the Voice with him.

Hearthunter told them that they could either walk on slowly or they could come with him. Both the girls decided to follow him, as they did not know where they would find Miraclekid and certainly did not want to enter Newchurch without Hearthunter.

As they climbed up the steep, grass-covered hill, the noise became louder and louder; and when they reached the top, Hearthunter cheered. The two girls could not believe their eyes.

At the bottom of the hill they saw a very large stage with enormous speakers at either side. On the stage stood four Littlekids. Two had guitars in their hands; one was playing a very large golden drum kit and the fourth was leaping around the stage twirling a microphone stand, looking like an overgrown drum majorette.

'What on earth are they?' shouted Rhoda as they descended the hill towards them and the noise reached an ear-shattering level.

'Well, they probably like to think they are musicians,' Hearthunter shouted back over the racket. 'Why I am so excited,' he continued, 'is because even though on first hearing they do not sound brilliant, I know the Voice is always on the look-out for people with some sort of musical ability that he can train up.'

'But they have no audience,' observed Harmony, also joining in the shouting.

'They don't need an audience,' laughed Hearthunter, recognising the style of music they were trying to play. 'They only play for their own ego. They think they are superior to anything else around, especially girls.'

As they approached the stage totally unnoticed by the performers, Hearthunter told them to try and listen to the words of the song they were singing. It was hard to recognise them with the accompanying din, but they did manage to pick out some of them.

> We hate chicks, yeah,
> Their brains are missin'.
> They're good for work, yeah,
> And for kissin'.
> But chicks they love us, yeah,
> They need us bad,
> 'Cos we're the best things, yeah,
> They ever had.
> 'Cos we're the best things, yeah,
> They ever had, Yeah, Yeah, Yeah ...

'What a load of chauvinistic rubbish!' shouted Rhoda angrily. Seeing a socket at the foot of the stage, she walked straight to it and pulled out the plug.

It took a few minutes before the band realised that they had now gone into a drum solo and that no noise was coming out of their amplifiers. The one who was shouting out the words put down his microphone stand, then rushed to the drummer and told him to stop playing. 'Something's wrong!' he shrieked.

The drummer was enjoying himself far too much to stop,

however, and his thrashing continued till he was pushed off his stool and was seen rolling around the stage on the floor. In no time the two guitarists joined in, and all four starting hitting and fighting each other.

Eventually everything went quiet as the arguing died down and Hearthunter, Harmony and Rhoda climbed up on the stage and walked towards them.

'Don't they look weird?' whispered Rhoda as she looked at their waist-length hair, dark sunglasses, leather jackets and skin-tight leather jeans to match. The leather was decorated with vicious-looking studs and chains. 'They need to look like that because they think it gives them a macho image,' whispered Hearthunter.

The microphone man, obviously the leader, walked over to the three Children of the Voice and pulled his hair out of his sunglasses to see who was there.

'Oi! Wot's your game?' he shouted, looking at them. 'Wos it one of you wot pulled our plug out?'

'Yes, I did,' retorted Rhoda very boldly. 'Just who do you think you are to sing such rubbish about girls?'

'Who are we?' said the singer, laughing. 'Did you hear that, boys?' he yelled to the rest of the band as they all straightened their dishevelled clothes and got off the floor.

'We only happen to be the heaviest, most famous, most wicked trash metal band in the Bigwideworld.' He then started his big introduction as though he were facing an audience of thousands.

'OK, you bozos. Right on, yeah! On drums we have *the* master of percussion ... Stix Insect!' Seeing there was no audience reaction or applause, he continued, '*The* unforgettable genius on bass guitar is ... uh—' temporarily forgetting his name '—Oh yeah ... Tuneless Wonder!' Still no applause. 'And the fastest fingers in the West on lead guitar, may I present to you ... Twang Fretfull!' Utter silence.

'And last but not least, mister wailing wall of sound himself ... yours truly ... Mac Throatsore!'

The band politely clapped their leader. 'Thank you, thank you, thank you, fans,' he shouted with all the panache of a mega-mega-star. 'Enough, enough,' he continued with his arms raised, long after the band had stopped applauding him anyway.

'Put all those four together and what have you got?' he said, building to a final big crescendo.

'Oh get on with it,' whispered Harmony, thinking they should be well on their way to Newchurch by now.

'Headbangers of the Bigwideworld we bring to you *the* loudest, heaviest, most digusting, scruffiest, most controversial, most wicked metal band sound of all time ... *'The ... Daisy Chains!'*

At this point all four members of the band leaped around the stage deliriously cheering, shouting and applauding themselves. After five minutes they all sat down, exhausted. (Obviously their self-admiration had worn them out, Harmony explained to Rhoda.)

'Well, it's great to meet you guys,' said Hearthunter, now taking over and ignoring the girls' comments. After introducing himself and his two friends, he started to explain that life was more than just loud music and putting girls down. He explained they could become brand new clean Littlekids if only they started loving the Voice instead of themselves.

Although Stix, Tuneless, Twang and Mac were not the most intelligent of Littlekids he had ever met, they listened with great interest as Hearthunter was now getting into top gear and explaining all about the Voice and how he went through terrible pain and suffering because he loved Littlekids like them.

'Yeah, but does he love our music?' interrupted Stix, who was even slower than the rest at catching on.

'I'm sure the Voice loves all kinds of music, including yours,' continued Hearthunter, 'but the problem is that a lot of Littlekids who play your kind of music are very much under the influence of the Enemy Superpower. And certainly you'd need to change the words of your songs.'

'Let me put it another way,' concluded Hearthunter. 'Both your lifestyle and your music are self-indulgent. If you want to become Children of the Voice, you stop doing just what you want to do and you start living to please the Voice. He must come before your music, your image and even your personal ambitions for fame.'

As the Voice was speaking to the four musicians at the same time as Hearthunter, it didn't take the band long to realise that they were really missing out. There on that vast stage they knelt down before the presence of the Voice and asked him to make them his children.

Hearthunter then explained that they now needed to go to the Voice's Training Module to learn more about the Voice; he gave them directions on how to get there. 'I'd take your instruments with you, if I were you,' he explained. 'The Voice will always use a talent as long as it's within his control.'

As Hearthunter, Harmony and Rhoda jumped off the stage and headed back to the Newchurch path, Mac shouted after them. 'Hey, just two more heavy questions I wanna lay on you guys.'

'What are they?' replied Hearthunter.

'The first is ...' he began, looking very embarrassed, 'could you tell us what a chick looks like? I don't think we'd know one if we saw one.'

'We are girls,' shouted Harmony and Rhoda, leaping up and down together, waving their arms in the air.

'Wow! Way out, baby ...' gasped Mac in amazement. 'You're much better than I would have guessed. In fact, you're human, just like us. I was always under the impression

96

that you were just sort of ... very uncool, unintelligent animals.'

'Well from now on you had better start respecting girls as people and stop treating them like "uncool, unintelligent animals," said Harmony.

'Yeah, baby, right on!' said Mac. 'The other question is this: do you think the Voice will find our name "The Daisy Chains" too uncool, way out or offensive?'

Hearthunter tried to stop himself bursting into laughter. 'Ah no, I think that the Voice might just be able to cope with such a controversial name,' he said.

The band was obviously thrilled, and Hearthunter, Harmony and Rhoda set off back over the hill. 'A worthwhile intermission,' said Hearthunter, excited as always at the opportunity of introducing Littlekids to the Voice. 'Who knows? One day they may be our worship band in Newchurch.'

'Yes, if there is any Newchurch still left to be part of,' sighed Harmony, grasping hold of Rhoda's hand.

'I guess you're right,' said Hearthunter thoughtfully. 'I think we should forget about trying to find Miraclekid and make our way straight to Newchurch.'

The others agreed, and away they went, singing the Littlekids' Marching Song.

14

Locked up—in a Lock-up Situation

Although the sun was shining brightly and it was the middle of the afternoon, Little Christian and Angela were surprised that the streets were deserted as they walked into Newchurch.

I wonder where everyone is? thought Little Christian. He had never known a time when there were not loads of happy, noisy younger Littlekids running around playing all over the place.

Little did they know that although they could see no one, many little eyes were well hidden but firmly focused on them.

'It's all so different from when we left ... and what's that over there?' said Angela.

Little Christian looked to where she was pointing and saw a huge, half-constructed mansion. 'I've no idea,' he said. 'Perhaps there has been a flood of new people and they are having to build some new accommodation.'

'Let's go and 'ave a look at it,' suggested Angela.

As they got closer, they at last saw life and movement. 'Look, there are some of the adults,' said Angela excitedly, and they both ran over, shouting in the direction of their friends.

'We're back!' shouted Little Christian and Angela as they ran up to the workers. But the adults just ignored them.

'What's going on?' shouted Little Christian. 'We're your friends. Please stop what you're doing, and let's talk.'

Again everyone just carried on working and treated Angela and Little Christian as though they were not there.

'Let's go and see if Buddy and Harmony are in the church office. Maybe they will explain to us what is happening.'

As they approached the office door they saw a gold plaque on it which had the words 'HEAVY SHEPHERD: PRIVATE' written in large letters for all to see.

Little Christian felt his stomach churn. 'O, Voice,' he said, 'there is something desperately wrong.' And as he prayed, he turned the handle and pushed the door open.

Angela and Little Christian could not believe their eyes. Seated there facing each other were three surprised Littlekids they had never seen before. On what used to be his desk were a pack of cards and piles of money, and the office was full of cigar smoke.

'What's the meaning of this invasion?' demanded the

largest of the Littlekids standing up and looking very important. 'Why are you not out working on the mansion with the rest of the Newagechurch of the Heavy Shepherd?'

'What in the name of all that's good are you talking about?' shouted Little Christian, looking at them angrily. 'Who are you? Where are Buddy and Harmony, and what do you think you're doing smoking and gambling in my office?'

'Now listen here,' said Dodgy Prophet, standing up next to his friend Heavy. 'No one talks to our leader like that and gets away with it. That's a punishable offence.'

Namit also stood up to throw his weight into the confrontation. 'Dodgy's right, pal, you have overstepped the mark. I suggest you apologise and get back to work.'

Little Christian was furious. 'Do you realise who I am? I'm Little Christian, the founder of Newchurch. What have you done to it?' he yelled as he rushed towards them, grabbed hold of his desk, and threw it across the room sending cards and money flying in every direction. A photograph fell out of the desk drawer and dropped onto the floor right in front of them.

'It's them,' whispered Heavy. 'Look, that's their photo!'

The three Enemy superbreeds stood petrified as they realised that although there was only one of him and three of them, he seemed much more powerful than they were. Angela stood back by the door and was also a little frightened as she had never seen Little Christian this angry before.

'Name yourselves,' snapped Little Christian, 'and then I want some answers out of you.'

Just as the scared and shaking trio were about to confess all, Little Christian heard a short cry and spun round to see that a fourth Littlekid had quietly crept in and had grabbed hold of Angela. He was now painfully twisting her arm behind her back.

'So we are having a little bit of trouble are we, gentlemen? Perhaps I can be of assistance to you. Now, grab Little Christian and tie him up. If he resists I will break Angela's arm off.'

Heavy, Dodgy and Namit looked very relieved to see that Percy Cutor had arrived.

'Well done, Percy,' exclaimed Heavy. 'We were just about to tackle him ourselves, weren't we, lads? We weren't scared of these Littlekids, even if one of them is Little Christian. Now come on, lads, do as Percy says. Tie him up.'

Percy smiled an evil grin and didn't even bother wasting his breath to call Heavy a liar. Little Christian offered no resistance; he knew that if he did Angela would get hurt.

'Now then, Angela, I want you to turn around slowly and look at me,' said Percy.

She had yet to see who was painfully hurting her, but as she turned and looked at him Little Christian saw her face go a whiter shade of pale. She froze with fear and started to tremble.

'So we meet again, Angela? And isn't that nice—you do recognise your old friend—once seen never forgotten I guess. How do you like my nice new name, "Percy Cutor"? So much more subtle than the name I had when we last met—what was it? Oh yes, The Pain Inflictor.'

'I am sure you realise though, my dear, as I hold your arm, the name may have changed but my job remains the same. I must admit that seeing you here is an embarrassment to me. I thought that you would never recover from my last onslaught. Still, this time I'll make sure I do my job properly.'

'Please don't 'urt me again,' cried Angela, tears running down her cheeks.

'You touch her and you are history, pal,' screamed Little Christian from underneath the mountain of ropes.

'Brave words, Little Christian, but I'm afraid you're in no condition to dish out threats. I'll tell you what I will do though, seeing as I'm a fair Littlekid. In my pocket I have a contract. Just sign it and I will let you go and leave you both alone.'

'What will we be signing?' asked Little Christian.

'Well, not much really,' said Percy. 'It' s just a simple matter of saying that you deny the existence of the Voice and swear allegiance to the Enemy Superpowers. Many greater than you have signed it in the past.'

'Never!' screamed Little Christian and Angela together. 'That would be the last thing we would ever do,' continued Little Christian.

'It very probably will be,' smiled Percy wickedly. 'Right lads, bring them over to my prison.'

'But we haven't got a prison,' remarked Heavy.

'No you haven't got a prison, Heavy,' argued Percy, 'but I have. Why do you think you have not seen much of me since I arrived? I've been preparing for this day for a long time.'

Having tied the fearful Angela up as well, Percy and Heavy dragged them up the street till they came to a side door in the hospital. There they walked along a corridor until they came to two very stout wooden doors facing each other. Percy unlocked them and pushed Angela into one and Little Christian into the other. Then he locked them both again.

'Right,' said Percy, 'I'll leave them for a few hours to reconsider my proposition. If the answer is still negative, I will get on and do what has to be done.' He grinned.

Both Angela and Little Christian sat in the dark unable to see a thing. Although they both felt very frightened, they both instinctively began to talk to the Voice.

There was no lock on the outside hospital door and as

the four superbreeds walked back to the office they didn't notice a younger Littlekid dart around the corner of the hospital, creep through the outside door and run to the door where Little Christian and Angela were being held captive.

15

A Light at the Beginning of the Tunnel

The remnant of Littlekids left in Newchurch lived in fear. Having seen how Heavy Shepherd had dealt with Harmony and Rhoda was bad enough, but things had got even worse. Tiff Withallsorts' house was still packed with adults who were planning a rebellion. Some were trying to change the name of Newagechurch, and all were thinking of ways to change the leadership.

When Tiff had collected a really committed group of rebels, she popped into the office and told Heavy all about it, making sure that she also gave him a list of all their names. In no time at all they were gathered up and banished to the Bigwideworld and warned that if they came back it would be the last thing they would ever do.

Although Tiff Withallsorts had tipped him off, Heavy didn't like or trust her because she had betrayed him by stirring everything up to start with. He arranged for his faithful followers Dodgy and Namit to see that she had a fatal accident while being escorted on a sight-seeing tour around the quick-drying concrete forming the foundations of an extension to his mansion.

Heavy held a very moving funeral service for her, explaining that she had been like a foundation stone to his work, which he was sure that she would have been proud of. But all the remaining Children of the Voice knew that she had been murdered, and their fears grew.

Every night adults would creep out under the protection of the darkness and run off into the Bigwideworld, but like sheep without a shepherd they had no idea where they were going. It was into this depleted, fearful atmosphere that Little Christian and Angela had arrived. Little wonder that everyone had been afraid to talk to them.

But although everyone seemed to be leaving through the back of the town, no one noticed three more creep in through the front. Hearthunter, Harmony and Rhoda quietly made their way into one of the many deserted houses and after speaking to the Voice opened their Manuals for a read while they waited for the right time to move.

'Oi! Little Christian, is that you?'

Little Christian stumbled through the darkness of his cell to where the voice was coming from. 'Who is it?' he whispered through the door.

'I'm a Littlekid,' the voice replied. 'My name is Ivor, Ivor Future.'

'I thought all you Littlekids had left months ago?' Little Christian said, surprised.

'No, we've just kept in hiding, waiting for you to return,' said Ivor.

Little Christian's fear went as he could see that the Voice was already answering his prayers. 'Listen, I know you can't get me out of here, but where are Buddy and Harmony?'

Ivor explained that Harmony had been thrown out of Newchurch for rebellion, while Buddy had cracked up, being full of guilt that he had allowed the evil leaders to take over. He was now in another part of the hospital suffering from a spiritual breakdown.

Little Christian was so angry at what the Enemy Superpowers had been up to that he nearly swore, but just in time he refrained and remembered that he must control himself and his language even in times like these. 'Listen, Ivor, where are you all hiding?' he asked.

'We are in the basement of the main building, right underneath the church office,' Ivor said.

'I didn't know it had a basement,' said Little Christian in amazement.

'No, and neither do those evil leaders,' chuckled Ivor.

'Well, wait there for me. I'll be out of here shortly. The Voice has told me so. One last thing, Ivor—try and get into the other part of the hospital and tell Buddy that I'm back.'

'He won't be any use. I'm afraid he's gone beyond help,' said Ivor sadly.

'Don't you believe it, Ivor. He has not gone beyond the Voice's help. So when you see him, tell those feelings of guilt and failure to leave him alone. Now, quickly, off you go and do as I say.'

Angela had not been able to hear any of the conversation Little Christian and Ivor had just had. Sitting shivering in the darkness, all she could see was the face of Percy the Pain Inflictor, and all the old hurts started to be relived in her mind. She started to cry uncontrollably, holding herself so tightly that her body started to bruise.

The hospital door opened, and the sound of Percy's boots echoed along the corridor. Hearing the sobbing coming from Angela's cell, he guessed that the memory of the pain he had already inflicted would be enough to having her screaming to sign the contract within the hour.

He opened Little Christian's door, dragged him out and pushed him into another room just a few yards away. 'This, Little Christian, is my studio,' he said with pride. 'I bet Angela never told you what she had to suffer, did she? Well, she won't have to now, because you can experience the joys of it all for yourself.' He tied Little Christian in a chair and then took hold of some headphones.

'What are you going to do to me?' asked Little Christian, still feeling brave. 'Beat me, hit me or worse?'

Percy laughed. 'Nothing as primitive as physical torture, Little Christian. It's a fact that bodily pain seems to make the Children of the Voice become even more stubborn and less likely to sign the contract. No, this is called *spiritual* torture.

'For the next few days you will not be allowed to sleep. I am going to put some headphones on you and then play you some nice cassettes. The first one will remind you of all the things you have done wrong in your life that you thought the Voice had forgiven and forgotten. We of course don't ever forgive or forget. We want to put all your past back into your mind, and by the time you have heard it a few hundred times you too will feel guilty and unforgiven. The second tape reminds you of all those times that the Voice did not answer your prayers, or sometimes answered them in a way that you were not happy with. Again, after a few hundred hearings you will be totally convinced that the Voice is unreliable and does not really care about you at all.

'And finally the third and most important tape, from my perspective, is the one that tells you about all the advantages and all the fun that can be had when you are truly committed to the Enemy Superpowers. And now . . . I'll put the contract here in front of you. All you have to do is give me a wave when you want to sign it, and then I will stop the tape. Then you will be a free man.'

'I'll never sign it,' yelled Little Christian defiantly.

'Oh, I'm sure you will,' said Percy. 'Angela only got away last time because after many hours she looked so weak and thin that I thought she was going to die on me, and the last thing I needed was a Littlekid martyr. Being a fool, I thought that if I let her go she would die somewhere in the Bigwideworld from so-called natural causes. I still don't know where she found the strength from to find her way back to you.'

'Well I do,' shouted Little Christian. 'Her strength came from the Voice, where mine will come from, too.'

'Very well,' sneered Percy. Then, applauding sarcastically, he put Little Christian's headphones on. 'But I fear that as true as that may be for you, you may not have noticed that Angela isn't quite as strong as she once was. In just a short while you and she will have nothing in common, because she will have signed over to become one of us. Happy listening, Little Christian!'

Ivor Future crept into the ward where Buddy was lying. 'Buddy, wake up! Little Christian is back,' he whispered.

Buddy spoke some rubbish, then turned over.

'Buddy, listen to me—Little Christian is here, and he needs your help.'

Buddy covered his face with his hands and started to sob like a baby.

'OK, so you won't listen to me, will you? Well, have it

your way. Maybe you will listen to the Voice.' Ivor jumped up and stood on the bed next to the prostrate Buddy. He commanded with an authority in his voice that made the whole hospital shake: 'Buddy, I pray that by the power of the Voice you will be released from self-pity, guilt and failure and that they will no longer be part of you. Receive this. Buddy, you are one of the Children of the Voice.'

Buddy immediately went still and quiet, then slowly lifted his head and looked at Ivor. 'Thank you,' he said slowly and quietly. 'Now please pass me my Manual and my clothes. We've a war to fight!'

16

Some You Win—but Lots You Lose

Buddy crept through the side door of the hospital, the Voice having already given him his instructions. He put his ear next to the first door but could hear nothing. Peeping through the key-hole he saw a muscley Littlekid he did not recognise walking around the room with his fingers in his ears while his friend Little Christian was tied to a chair with some headphones on, singing at the top of his voice the Littlekids' Marching Song.

'Well, Little Christian seems to be enjoying himself, but singing was never his strong point,' he thought. Quietly he went away from the door; then, moving farther down the corridor, he heard loud sobbing. 'Thank you, Voice,' he said. 'This must be the room where she is, but the door's sure to be locked. How am I going to get in?'

The Voice told him to grab the handle and pull. To his surprise he realised the door was undone. 'That must have happened when Ivor prayed for me and the building shook,' he thought.

Opening the door, he whispered Angela's name. 'Leave me alone,' she cried, 'I'll never stop followin' the Voice, whatever ya do to me.'

'Of course you won't, Angela—and all I want to do is to pray for you.'

Angela lifted her head out of her hands and through her red tearful eyes saw Buddy. 'Buddy, is that really you?' Pulling herself out of her heap she ran towards the door and hugged him. 'Where 'ave ya bin 'idin'?'

'Um, that's a long story,' said Buddy, looking a bit embarrassed. 'But just at this moment I've more important things to do than to talk about me . . . listen, Angela, you are desperately in need of some prayer for healing. You really should have talked to us, your friends, when you first went through your horrific experience with Percy Cutor. Those kinds of fears, hurts and memories do not disappear with time—they just fester away under the surface until they can raise their ugly heads again.'

'I'm sorry,' said Angela. 'I know ye'r right. I wouldn't be in the state that I am now if I 'ad bin willin' to be 'onest with ya, and 'ad allowed ya and the Voice to speak to me.'

Buddy stopped her talking by taking the Manual out of his pocket and reading some exciting words of encouragement. Then he started to pray. He asked that she would know healing from all she had been through, and that the Voice would bring her back to full health and strength. As he prayed and she received the prayer, he could feel the power of the Voice doing exactly what Buddy had asked. Within minutes the prayers of asking turned to prayers of thanks, and together they spent some time worshipping the Voice.

Dusk fell and the cloak of darkness covered Newchurch. The coming of the night also heralded the departure of the last adults, who drifted sadly out into the nowhere land of the Bigwideworld.

Heavy Shepherd, Dodgy Prophet and Namit Claimit stood happily in the shadow of a building and watched the final exodus, while a jubilant Greedy Gutrot and Professor Mindwarpt hid behind a rock and watched the sad refugees enter their evil domain.

'Nearly there,' said Mindwarpt, rubbing his grisled hands together. 'Newchurch is dead, and in an hour or so's time there will be no more Children of the Voice.'

'Excellent,' smiled Gutrot. 'Well done, Professor. I feel that as a final gesture—a kind of nail in the coffin sort of thing—it would be most helpful if you could programme your little superbreeds to burn down what's left of Newchurch.' He sniffed at his scorched clothes. 'After all, I know first-hand just how destructive fire can be. Let's give that Little Christian a taste of his own medicine and see how he likes it!'

'No sooner said than done,' said the obedient Mindwarpt.

Gutrot continued looking at Newchurch in the distance. Then with an even broader and uglier grin he told the Professor that as soon as the last Littlekid was in his power, he would send back the wandering adults so they could rebuild the city of Oldchurch. 'I'd much rather have them all in one place where we can keep an eye on them,' he concluded. Mindwarpt agreed. Meanwhile, Heavy, Dodgy and Namit wasted no time in obeying the Professor's commands. Soon most of Newchurch was a fiery furnace, and they laughed at the destruction they were causing.

Just as they felt that their job was completed and it was time to return to their maker, they heard a voice they recognised.

'So we meet again, do we?'

Heavy, Dodgy and Namit spun around and came face-to-face with Hearthunter, Harmony and Rhoda.

'Well, I'll be ...' said Heavy. 'Not you two girls back again! But you're a bit late, aren't you? We have just destroyed Newchurch.'

'Maybe you have,' said Hearthunter. 'That can be rebuilt, but you will never destroy the Children of the Voice. And we aim to stop you trying.'

'O, come on now,' laughed Heavy. 'Do you really think you and two girls are any match for the three of us? Get them, lads.'

Immediately the Children of the Voice stepped forward and commanded in the power of the Voice that the three evil Littlekids should freeze. Although it did sound a rather strange command with the heat of all the burning buildings around them, it worked. The only part of their beings they could move was their mouths; they were imprisoned in their own bodies and just stood like statues.

'Now we just need to find out from the Voice what he wants us to do with you,' said Hearthunter, staring at them one at a time.

Inside the hospital, Buddy had finished praying with Angela and after their time of worship it was like their batteries had been fully recharged.

'Right, let's go,' said Buddy.

They walked down the corridor until they reached the studio. 'Stand back,' said Buddy with more authority in his voice than Angela had ever heard him use before. 'Let's see this wicked Littlekid jump!' And with that he lifted his foot and kicked the door down.

Percy really did jump in surprise. Then he leaped to his feet, but before he could do anything to retaliate he also heard the words, 'In the name of the Voice, freeze'—and he stood motionless with his eyes glaring and mouth wide open.

They quickly took off Little Christian's headphones and untied him. He hugged Buddy and Angela, and Buddy asked him how he felt and if he needed some prayer. Little Christian smiled, 'I always need prayer,' he said, 'but those tapes couldn't affect me as I just kept singing the Voice's song. I think my singing affected old Percy more than his tapes affected me,' he joked. 'Right now, it's time to purge Newchurch of these infiltrating Littlekids,' he said. 'All is not lost yet.'

17
The End?

Little Christian had spoken too soon. As they dragged the stiff Percy Cutor out onto the street they all gasped as they saw the night sky lit up by blazing buildings.

'No!' screamed Little Christian. 'We are too late. They have destroyed Newchurch.'

The only buildings that were not well ablaze by now, apart from the hospital, were the church office and the adjoining meeting hall. Everything else crackled and flamed furiously.

They continued dragging Percy down the street towards the office, weeping at the destruction of all their hard work in Newchurch. Then they suddenly saw three more people dragging three other stiff Littlekids down the street. Although it was exciting to meet their friends, the reunion was marred by the crashing timber of the town burning around them.

'Where have all the Children of the Voice gone?' Little Christian enquired, bewildered.

'They have all left to go back to the Bigwideworld and Oldchurch,' said Harmony sadly.

'Yes, I think we are the only ones left. Nobody will trust a Newchurch again,' added Rhoda.

Heavy Shepherd was lying with the other evil superbreeds in a line on the ground, and as he didn't want to be terminated he had one last plan for survival. Summoning all the emotion he could manage, he suddenly burst into a flood of tears which made the Children of the Voice turn and look at him. 'Woe is me,' he cried out. 'I've done wrong. No, we've all done wrong. Please forgive us. Let us go in peace. We really have seen the error of our ways—' he lied '—and we feel a stint at the Voice's Training Module would put us back on the straight and narrow. There I can learn to be a *good* shepherd,' he continued, 'Dodgy a good Prophet, Namit a good faith man and Percy a good ... well just good.' (He stopped awkwardly, having failed to think of anything that Percy could be good at except hurting people.)

Percy, Dodgy and Namit thought he had flipped his lid until they saw Heavy wink at them through his teary eye.

'Yes, we have all been wicked,' they quickly joined in, 'but surely you must forgive four repentant Littlekids? After all, haven't we all done wrong at one time or another?'

And let he who is without wrong chuck the first brick,' sobbed the blubbering Namit, who was a better actor than all the rest put together.

Little Christian felt the Voice prompt him that they were lying and he must not be deceived.

Buddy felt sorry for them as did Hearthunter, Harmony and Rhoda; but Little Christian felt a righteous anger welling up inside him against them. There was something unusually evil about them, but he couldn't put his finger on what it was.

'Well, the Manual does say that we must forgive Littlekids wot are really sorry,' quoted Angela.

'So it's all agreed, then,' said Buddy, taking control. 'We shall ask the Voice to release them, and then we'll let them go to the Training Module.'

'Thanks,' said the Enemy Littlekids, their tears evaporating as quickly as they had appeared.

'We'll be eternally grateful,' grinned Dodgy.

'Not so quick,' Little Christian butted in. 'I can't forgive them. They have wrecked lives and wrecked Newchurch. They are evil and must be destroyed.'

Before anyone could move he rushed over, grabbed a burning log and threw it at the four lying on the floor. 'You seem to love fire. Well, see how you get on with this,' he yelled defiantly. Within seconds they we all ablaze, but they made no noise.

Angela, Harmony and Rhoda screamed with horror while Buddy and Hearthunter tried in vain to dowse the flames. Within minutes it was all over for Heavy, Dodgy, Namit and Percy. They just lay in a smouldering heap.

The Children of the Voice just stared. No one said a word.

Eventually Buddy walked over to Little Christian. 'What have you done?' he whispered to him. 'You have killed four Littlekids. You've tried to do the Voice's work for him.' These Littlekids had repented.'

'But I felt it was right,' argued Little Christian. 'I couldn't let them just walk away.'

119

'Feelings ain't wot ya go on, Little Christian,' said Angela, 'Ye'r a let-down to all the Children of the Voice,' she said with angry tears. 'Just fink, I fought we might 'ave 'ad a future togever. I fought I loved ya, but I could never be married to a murderer. I never want ta talk to ya again.' She wept, turning away from him.

'Listen, they were not normal Littlekids. There was something weird about them. Surely you could all see that. I had to destroy them—I'm sure the Voice was telling me to,' explained Little Christian.

'You are as violent as they are,' said Hearthunter. 'You have their blood on your hands. I'm afraid you're no longer part of us. I suggest you leave. Newchurch is no home for you. You can no longer be known as one of the Children of the Voice,' said Hearthunter softly, putting his hand on Little Christian's shoulder. 'I'm sorry it had to end like this. Maybe in a few years' time if you really repent the Voice will give you another chance. Little Christian, go, and may the Voice have mercy on you.'

All went silent as Little Christian turned away from them.

He walked down the middle of the street with houses that he had helped build just two years ago burning on either side of him. He was broken-hearted and wept uncontrollably. 'I've lost Newchurch, my friends and the girl I really did love. Why did I have to kill them, and why can't I feel sorry that I did so?' he cried. Only the Voice listened to him.

By the time Little Christian had disappeared out of sight, all the other Children of the Voice were weeping. They were sorry to lose their leader and their best friend, but they knew they had to stand by what was right.

Suddenly Rhoda's tears stopped flowing, and she screamed as she saw a face peer round from the office. Then another appeared, then another.

'Look!' shouted Buddy, wiping his eyes, '—Littlekids, come out and join us.'

'Is it safe?' said Ivor whom Buddy instantly recognised.

'Yes, it's all over,' he announced as the numerous Littlekids poured out of the cellar and wandered around looking at the charred, smouldering remains surrounding them.

'We didn't like to come out. We were waiting for Little Christian to give us the OK. Where is he, anyway?' asked Ivor.

'I'm afraid Little Christian has done a very wicked deed,' explained Buddy as gently as he could. Heavy Shepherd, Percy, Dodgy and Namit all confessed and were sorry for the wrong they had done, but Little Christian couldn't forgive them and killed them. Whatever anyone has done, human life is sacred and it is not for us to take it away.'

Suddenly a floppy thing was thrown at his feet.

'You fools!' yelled Ivor Future angrily. 'Is it murder to destroy an Enemy robot?' he asked, pointing to the mechanical remains of Lucy Morals. 'You've condemned your leader for destroying the Enemy Superpower's machines!'

Buddy, Harmony, Hearthunter, Rhoda and Angela could not believe their eyes.

'Robots!' exclaimed Hearthunter. 'You mean they were not normal Littlekids? Oh, no, I don't believe it.'

They all ran and looked at the charred remains of the four Littlekids, and sure enough all that was left was a pile of burned nuts, bolts and metal.

'Enemy Superpower robots sent in to invade Newchurch and destroy us and our leader—you have certainly allowed them to do that,' continued Ivor.

'So the Voice did tell Little Christian ta destroy these evil machines and we didn't believe 'im?' whispered Angela. She began to cry again. 'Oh, no. Wot 'ave I done ta the one wot I really care fer.'

'We have not only broken and condemned to exile one of the Voice's greatest Littlekids, but we have also sent him away with the guilt of a murderer,' said Hearthunter, falling to his knees in shame.

'But will he ever come back?' cried Rhoda.

'Would *you* after the way he has been treated?' Buddy asked.

'If I run, I may be able ta catch 'im,' suggested Angela, sobbing.

'That won't be any use, I'm afraid,' continued Buddy. 'You'll never find him out there in the dark, and even if you did I doubt if he will believe you or want to see any of us again. We now have to live under a cloud of guilt, and even if we try to rebuild Newchurch, it won't have—and never will have—its rightful leader.'

Angela, Buddy, Hearthunter, Harmony, Rhoda, Ivor and all the rest of the younger Littlekids knelt down in the road and prayed for the Voice's protection on Little Christian; also that one day he might forgive them and come back to them.

Greedy Gutrot and Professor Mindwarpt were dancing around, over the moon at the outcome. 'It couldn't have come out better if we had planned it ourselves,' they laughed. 'I mean we had casualties and lost Heavy Shepherd, Lucy Morals, Dodgy Prophet, Namit Claimit, Tiff Withallsorts and Percy Cutor—but look what we have achieved. You can always build more robots, but they will never be able to rebuild Newchurch, not while Little Christian is wandering depressed and alone all over the Bigwideworld. Yes ... Little Christian and the Children of the Voice are gone for ever!' shrieked Gutrot with a shake of his huge belly.

Then they went quiet as they heard a voice cut through the air above them. Like a double-edged sword it threw them both to the ground.

'In the name of the Voice I call fire down from heaven. Burn them, Voice. Burn them up and all the evil they represent.'

'Oh no, not fire again,' shouted Gutrot as two firebolts shot out of the sky. Instantly he and Mindwarpt were reduced to just two pools of mess on the rocks.

'Well that will slow down their celebrations for a bit,' declared Miraclekid looking at his friend. 'By the way, I must teach you how to call down fire from heaven properly, so you'll never have to resort to using an old piece of burning wood again. Just think of the agro that could have saved you,' he chuckled.

'Now, come on,' Miraclekid added, 'let's go back and join the others ... we've got a lot of rebuilding to do.'

And he and Little Christian set off ... back to Newchurch.

COMING SOON TO A BOOKSHOP NEAR YOU—
CHILDREN OF THE VOICE 3

THE LITTLEKIDS MARCHING SONG

Triumphantly

Ishmael

There is no one else a-round, in the air or on the ground who has the pow-er, has the pow-er of the voice. So you en-e-my su-per pow'rs in your de-feat-ed fi-nal hours, we com-mand you to leave you have no choice you have no choice— and we speak in the au-thor-i-ty of the voice.

124

Children Of The Voice

by Ishmael

He was Little Trouble by name, because the grown-ups who ruled Oldchurch thought he must be that by nature. Keep the Littlehorrors out of Real Church, and, when they show signs of growing up, leave them to the Bigwideworld.

But Little Trouble wants to hear the Voice—the One everyone says they go to church for. Fed up with Oldchurch, he sets off on his quest, passing on his way through Crosscountry, Wastetime University and the alluring Securicity.

He has a lot to learn, some new friends to make, and some surprising enemies. And at the end of it all, he has to go back to Oldchurch...

This is Ishmael's first work of fiction, blending the mood of *Pilgrim's Progress* and *Animal Farm*. Fun for any age, it speaks volumes about the divisions we so often try to maintain between God's older children and his younger ones.

Also by Ishmael in Kingsway paperback: *The History of Ishmael Part One* and *Angels with Dirty Faces*.

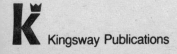

Kingsway Publications

The History of Ishmael

by Ian Smale

Ishmael—what do you make of him?

Don't think of an answer just now—suspend judgement for a while, and let him speak for himself.

Tongues before the 'charismatic movement'. Early rock 'n' roll at the Girl Guides. Life on the farm (it shouldn't happen to a choirboy). And the price of fame, the serious truth behind the humorous stage image.

It's all here, told as only Ishmael could tell it.

Kingsway Publications

Angels With Dirty Faces

by Ishmael

Ishmael loves children. Here's how—and why.

'Through all the years I've never known anyone who can so motivate children in worship, or lead them so securely into the things of the Spirit of God.'

—Jim Graham, Pastor,
Goldhill Baptist Church.

K
Kingsway Publications

 **Kingsway Publications**

Kingsway Publications publishes books to encourage spiritual values in the home, church and society. The list includes Bibles, popular paperbacks, more specialist volumes, booklets, and a range of children's fiction.

Kingsway Publications is owned by The Servant Trust, a Christian charity run by representatives of the evangelical church in Britain, committed to serving God in publishing and music.

For further information on the Trust, including details of how you may be able to support its work, please write to:

The Secretary
The Servant Trust
1 St Anne's Road
Eastbourne
East Sussex BN21 3UN
England